GULLIBLE'S TRAVELS, ETC.

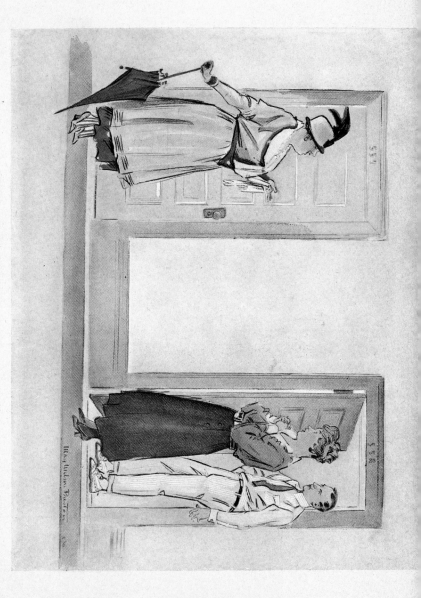

"Please see that they's some towels put in 559."

Gullible's Travels, Etc.

By
RING W. LARDNER

Author of
You Know Me, Al, etc.

Illustrated by
MAY WILSON PRESTON

INDIANAPOLIS
THE BOBBS-MERRILL COMPANY
PUBLISHERS

PRESS OF
BRAUNWORTH & CO.
BOOK MANUFACTURERS
BROOKLYN, N. Y.

CONTENTS

GULLIBLE'S TRAVELS, ETC.

Gullible's Travels, Etc.

CARMEN

WE was playin' rummy over to Hatch's, and Hatch must of fell in a bed of four-leaf clovers on his way home the night before, because he plays rummy like he does everything else; but this night I refer to you couldn't beat him, and besides him havin' all the luck my Missus played like she'd been bought off, so when we come to settle up we was plain seven and a half out. You know who paid it. So Hatch says:

"They must be some game you can play."

"No," I says, "not and beat you. I can run two blocks w'ile you're stoopin' over to start, but if we was runnin' a foot race between each other, and suppose I was leadin' by eighty yards, a flivver'd prob'ly come up and hit you in the back and bump you over the finishin' line ahead o' me."

So Mrs. Hatch thinks I'm sore on account o' the seven-fifty, so she says:

"It don't seem fair for us to have all the luck."

"Sure it's fair!" I says. "If you didn't have the luck, what would you have?"

"I know," she says; "but I don't never feel right winnin' money at cards."

"I don't blame you," I says.

"I know," she says; "but it seems like we should ought to give it back or else stand treat, either one."

"Jim's too old to change all his habits," I says.

"Oh, well," says Mrs. Hatch, "I guess if I told him to loosen up he'd loosen up. I ain't lived with him all these years for nothin'."

"You'd be a sucker if you did," I says.

So they all laughed, and when they'd quieted down Mrs. Hatch says:

"I don't suppose you'd feel like takin' the money back?"

"Not without a gun," I says. "Jim's pretty husky."

So that give them another good laugh; but finally she says:

"What do you say, Jim, to us takin' the money they lose to us and gettin' four tickets to some show?"

Jim managed to stay conscious, but he couldn't answer nothin'; so my Missus says:

"That'd be grand of you to do it, but don't think you got to."

Well, of course, Mrs. Hatch knowed all the w'ile she didn't have to, but from what my Missus says she could tell that if they really give us the invitation we wouldn't start no fight. So they talked it over between themself w'ile I and Hatch went out in the kitchen and split a pint o' beer, and Hatch done the pourin' and his best friend couldn't say he give himself the worst of it. So when we come back my Missus and Mrs. Hatch had it all framed that the Hatches

3

was goin' to take us to a show, and the next thing was what show would it be. So Hatch found the afternoon paper, that somebody'd left on the street-car, and read us off a list o' the shows that was in town. I spoke for the Columbia, but the Missus give me the sign to stay out; so they argued back and forth and finally Mrs. Hatch says:

"Let's see that paper a minute."

"What for?" says Hatch. "I didn't hold nothin' out on you."

But he give her the paper and she run through the list herself, and then she says:

"You did, too, hold out on us. You didn't say nothin' about the Auditorium."

"What could I say about it?" says Hatch. "I never was inside."

"It's time you was then," says Mrs. Hatch.

"What's playin' there?" I says.

"Grand op'ra," says Mrs. Hatch.

"Oh!" says my Missus. "Wouldn't that be wonderful?"

"What do you say?" says Mrs. Hatch to me.

"I think it'd be grand for you girls," I says. "I and Jim could leave you there and go down on Madison and see Charley Chaplin, and then come back after you."

"Nothin' doin'!" says Mrs. Hatch. "We'll pick a show that everybody wants to see."

Well, if I hadn't of looked at my Missus then we'd of been O. K. But my eyes happened to light on where she was settin' and she was chewin' her lips so's she wouldn't cry. That finished me. "I was just kiddin'," I says to Mrs. Hatch. "They ain't nothin' I'd like better than grand op'ra."

"Nothin' except gettin' trimmed in a rummy game," says Hatch, but he didn't get no rise.

Well, the Missus let loose of her lips so's she could smile and her and Mrs. Hatch got all excited, and I and Hatch pretended like we was excited too. So Hatch ast what night could we go, and Mrs. Hatch says that depended on what did we want to hear, because they changed the bill every day. So her and the Missus looked at the paper again and found out where

Friday night was goin' to be a big special night and the bill was a musical show called *Carmen,* and all the stars was goin' to sing, includin' Mooratory and Alda and Genevieve Farr'r, that was in the movies a w'ile till they found out she could sing, and some fella they called Daddy, but I don't know his real name. So the girls both says Friday night was the best, but Hatch says he would have to go to lodge that evenin'.

"Lodge!" says Mrs. Hatch. "What do you care about lodge when you got a chance to see Genevieve Farr'r in *Carmen?*"

"Chance!" says Hatch. "If that's what you call a chance, I got a chance to buy a thousand shares o' Bethlehem Steel. Who's goin' to pay for my chance?"

"All right," says Mrs. Hatch, "go to your old lodge and spoil everything!"

So this time it was her that choked up and made like she was goin' to blubber. So Hatch changed his mind all of a sudden and decided to disappoint the brother Owls. So all of us

was satisfied except fifty per cent., and I and
the Missus beat it home, and on the way she
says how nice Mrs. Hatch was to give us this
treat.

"Yes," I says, "but if you hadn't of had a
regular epidemic o' discardin' deuces and treys
Hatch would of treated us to groceries for a
week." I says: "I always thought they was
only twelve pitcher cards in the deck till I seen
them hands you saved up to-night."

"You lose as much as I did," she says.

"Yes," I says, "and I always will as long as
you forget to fetch your purse along."

So they wasn't no comeback to that, so we
went on home without no more dialogue.

Well, Mrs. Hatch called up the next night
and says Jim had the tickets boughten and we
was to be sure and be ready at seven o'clock
Friday night because the show started at eight.
So when I was down-town Friday the Missus
sent my evenin' dress suit over to Katzes' and
had it pressed up and when I come home it was
laid out on the bed like a corpse.

7

"What's that for?" I says.

"For the op'ra," she says. "Everybody wears them to the op'ra."

"Did you ask the Hatches what was they goin' to wear?" I says.

"No," says she. "They know what to wear without me tellin' them. They ain't goin' to the Auditorium in their nightgown."

So I clumb into the soup and fish, and the Missus spent about a hour puttin' on a dress that she could have left off without nobody knowin' the difference, and she didn't have time for no supper at all, and I just managed to surround a piece o' steak as big as your eye and spill some gravy on my clo'es when the bell rung and there was the Hatches.

Well, Hatch didn't have no more evenin' dress suit on than a kewpie. I could see his pants under his overcoat and they was the same old bay pants he'd wore the day he got mad at his kid and christened him Kenneth. And his shoes was a last year's edition o' the kind that's supposed to give your feet a chance, and

8

if his feet had of been the kind that takes
chances they was two or three places where they
could of got away without much trouble.

I could tell from the expression on Mrs.
Hatch's face when she seen our make-up that
we'd crossed her. She looked about as comf't-
able as a Belgium.

"Oh!" she says. "I didn't think you'd dress
up."

"We thought you would," says my Frau.

"We!" I says. "Where do you get that
'we'?"

"If it ain't too late we'll run in and change,"
says my Missus.

"Not me," I says. "I didn't go to all this
trouble and expense for a splash o' gravy.
When this here uniform retires it'll be to make
room for pyjamas."

"Come on!" says Hatch. "What's the difference? You can pretend like you ain't with
us."

"It don't really make no difference," says
Mrs. Hatch.

And maybe it didn't. But we all stood within whisperin' distance of each other on the car goin' in, and if you had a dollar for every word that was talked among us you couldn't mail a postcard from Hammond to Gary. When we got off at Congress my Missus tried to thaw out the party.

"The prices is awful high, aren't they?" she says.

"Outrageous," says Mrs. Hatch.

Well, even if the prices was awful high, they didn't have nothin' on our seats. If I was in trainin' to be a steeple jack I'd go to grand op'ra every night and leave Hatch buy my ticket. And where he took us I'd of been more at home in overalls and a sport shirt.

"How do you like Denver?" says I to the Missus, but she'd sank for the third time.

"We're safe here," I says to Hatch. "Them French guns can't never reach us. We'd ought to brought more bumbs."

"What did the seats cost?" I says to Hatch.

"One-fifty," he says.

"Very reasonable," says I. "One o' them aviators wouldn't take you more than half this height for a five-spot."

The Hatches had their overcoats off by this time and I got a look at their full costume. Hatch had went without his vest durin' the hot months and when it was alongside his coat and pants it looked like two different families. He had a pink shirt with prune-colored horizontal bars, and a tie to match his neck, and a collar that would of took care of him and I both, and them shoes I told you about, and burlap hosiery. They wasn't nothin' the matter with Mrs. Hatch except she must of thought that, instead o' dressin' for the op'ra, she was gettin' ready for Kenneth's bath.

And there was my Missus, just within the law, and me all spicked and spanned with my soup and fish and gravy!

Well, we all set there and tried to get the focus till about a half-hour after the show was billed to commence, and finally a Lilliputhian with a match in his hand come out and started up the orchestry and they played a few o' the hits and then the lights was turned out and up went the curtain.

Well, sir, you'd be surprised at how good we could hear and see after we got used to it. But the hearin' didn't do us no good—that is, the words part of it. All the actors had been smuggled in from Europe and they wasn't none o' them that could talk English. So all their songs was gave in different languages and I wouldn't of never knew what was goin' on only for Hatch havin' all the nerve in the world.

After the first act a lady that was settin' in front of us dropped somethin' and Hatch stooped over and picked it up, and it was one o' these here books they call a liberetto, and it's got all the words they're singin' on the stage wrote out in English.

So the lady begin lookin' all over for it and Hatch was goin' to give it back because he thought it was a shoe catalogue, but he happened to see at the top of it where it says "Price

25 Cents," so he tossed it in his lap and stuck his hat over it. And the lady kept lookin' and lookin' and finally she turned round and looked Hatch right in the eye, but he dropped down inside his collar and left her wear herself out. So when she'd gave up I says somethin' about I'd like to have a drink.

"Let's go," says Hatch.

"No," I says. "I don't want it bad enough to go back to town after it. I thought maybe we could get it sent up to the room."

"I'm goin' alone then," says Hatch.

"You're liable to miss the second act," I says.

"I'd never miss it," says Hatch.

"All right," says I. "I hope you have good weather."

So he slipped me the book to keep for him and beat it. So I seen the lady had forgot us, and I opened up the book and that's how I come to find out what the show was about. I read her all through, the part that was in English, before the curtain went up again, so when the second act begin I knowed what had came

off and what was comin' off, and Hatch and
Mrs. Hatch hadn't no idear if the show was
comical or dry. My Missus hadn't, neither, till
we got home and I told her the plot.

Carmen ain't no regular musical show where
a couple o' Yids comes out and pulls a few lines
o' dialogue and then a girl and a he-flirt sings
a song that ain't got nothin' to do with it.
Carmen's a regular play, only instead o' them
sayin' the lines, they sing them, and in for'n
languages so's the actors can pick up some loose
change offen the sale o' the liberettos. The
music was wrote by George S. Busy, and it
must of kept him that way about two mont's.
The words was either throwed together by the
stage carpenter or else took down by a stenographer outdoors durin' a drizzle. Anyway,
they ain't nobody claims them. Every oncet
in three or four pages they forget themself and
rhyme. You got to read each verse over two
or three times before you learn what they're
hintin' at, but the management gives you

plenty o' time to do it between acts and still sneak a couple o' hours' sleep.

The first act opens up somewheres in Spain, about the corner o' Chicago Avenue and Wells. On one side o' the stage they's a pill mill where the employees is all girls, or was girls a few years ago. On the other side they's a soldiers' garage where they keep the militia in case of a strike. In the back o' the stage they's a bridge, but it ain't over no water or no railroad tracks or nothin'. It's prob'ly somethin' the cat dragged in.

Well, the soldiers stands out in front o' the garage hittin' up some barber shops, and pretty soon a girl blows in from the hero's home town, Janesville or somewheres. She runs a few steps every little w'ile and then stops, like the rails was slippery. The soldiers sings at her and she tells them she's came to look for Don Joss that run the chop-suey dump up to Janesville, but when they shet down on him servin' beer he quit and joined the army. So the soldiers never heard o' the bird, but they all ask her if they won't do just as good, but she says nothin' doin' and skids off the stage. She ain't no sooner gone when the Chinaman from Janesville and some more soldiers and some alley rats comes in to help out the singin'. The book says that this new gang o' soldiers was sent on to relieve the others, but if anything happened to wear out the first ones it must of took place at rehearsal. Well, one o' the boys tells Joss about the girl askin' for him and he says: "Oh, yes; that must be the little Michaels girl from up in Wisconsin."

So pretty soon the whistle blows for noon and the girls comes out o' the pill mill smokin' up the mornin' receipts and a crowd o' the unemployed comes in to shoot the snipes. So the soldiers notices that Genevieve Farr'r ain't on yet, so they ask where she's at, and that's her cue. She puts on a song number and a Spanish dance, and then she slips her bouquet to the Chink, though he ain't sang a note since the whistle blowed. But now it's one o'clock and Genevieve and the rest o' the girls beats it back

to the coffin factory and the vags chases down
to the Loop to get the last home edition and
look at the want ads to see if they's any jobs
open with fair pay and nothin' to do. And the
soldiers mosey into the garage for a well-
earned rest and that leaves Don all alone on the
stage.

But he ain't no more than started on his next
song when back comes the Michaels girl. It
oozes out here that she's in love with the Joss
party, but she stalls and pretends like his
mother'd sent her to get the receipt for makin'
eggs *fo yung*. And she says his mother ast her
to kiss him and she slips him a dime, so he
leaves her kiss him on the scalp and he asks her
if she can stay in town that evenin' and see a
nickel show, but they's a important meetin' o'
the Maccabees at Janesville that night, so away
she goes to catch the two-ten and Don starts
in on another song number, but the rest o' the
company don't like his stuff and he ain't hardly
past the vamp when they's a riot.

It seems like Genevieve and one o' the chorus

girls has quarreled over a second-hand stick o'
gum and the chorus girl got the gum, but Genevieve relieved her of part of a earlobe, so they
pinch Genevieve and leave Joss to watch her
till the wagon comes, but the wagon's went out
to the night desk sergeant's house with a case
o' quarts and before it gets round to pick up
Genevieve she's bunked the Chink into settin'
her free. So she makes a getaway, tellin' Don
to meet her later on at Lily and Pat's place
acrost the Indiana line. So that winds up the
first act.

Well, the next act's out to Lily and Pat's,
and it ain't no Y. M. C. A. headquarters, but
it's a hang-out for dips and policemans. They's
a cabaret and Genevieve's one o' the performers, but she forgets the words to her first song
and winds up with tra-la-la, and she could of
forgot the whole song as far as I'm concerned,
because it wasn't nothin' you'd want to buy and
take along home.

Finally Pat comes in and says it's one o'clock
and he's got to close up, but they won't none

o' them make a move, and pretty soon they's
a live one blows into the joint and he's Eskimo
Bill, one o' the butchers out to the Yards. He's
got paid that day and he ain't never goin'
home. He sings a song and it's the hit o' the
show. Then he buys a drink and starts flirtin'
with Genevieve, but Pat chases everybody but
the performers and a couple o' dips that ain't
got nowheres else to sleep. The dips or stick-up
guys, or whatever they are, tries to get Genevieve to go along with them in the car w'ile
they pull off somethin', but she's still expectin'
the Chinaman. So they pass her up and blow,
and along comes Don and she lets him in, and
it seems like he'd been in jail for two mont's,
or ever since the end o' the first act. So he
asks her how everything has been goin' down
to the pill mill and she tells him that she's
quit and became a entertainer. So he says,
"What can you do?" And she beats time
with a pair o' chopsticks and dances the Chi-
nese Blues.

After a w'ile they's a bugle call somewhere

outdoors and Don says that means he's got to go back to the garage. So she gets sore and tries to bean him with a Spanish onion. Then he reaches inside his coat and pulls out the bouquet she give him in Atto First to show her he ain't changed his clo'es, and then the sheriff comes in and tries to coax him with a razor to go back to his job. They fight like it was the first time either o' them ever tried it and the sheriff's leadin' on points when Genevieve hollers for the dips, who dashes in with their gats pulled and it's good night, Mister Sheriff! They put him in moth balls and they ask Joss to join their tong. He says all right and they're all pretty well lit by this time and they've reached the singin' stage, and Pat can't get them to go home and he's scared some o' the Hammond people'll put in a complaint, so he has the curtain rang down.

Then they's a relapse of it don't say how long, and Don and Genevieve and the yeggs and their lady friends is all out in the country somewheres attendin' a Bohunk Sokol Verein picnic and Don starts whinin' about his old lady that he'd left up to Janesville.

"I wisht I was back there," he says.

"You got nothin' on me," says Genevieve. "Only Janesville ain't far enough. I wisht you was back in Hongkong."

So w'ile they're flatterin' each other back and forth, a couple o' the girls is monkeyin' with the pasteboards and tellin' their fortunes, and one o' them turns up a two-spot and that's a sign they're goin' to sing a duet. So it comes true and then Genevieve horns into the game and they play three-handed rummy, singin' all the w'ile to bother each other, but finally the fellas that's runnin' the picnic says it's time for the fat man's one-legged race and everybody goes offen the stage. So the Michaels girl comes on and is gettin' by pretty good with a song when she's scared by the noise o' the gun that's fired to start the race for the bay-window championship. So she trips back to her dressin'-room and then Don and Eskimo Bill put on a little slap-stick stuff.

When they first meet they're pals, but as soon as they get wise that the both o' them's bugs over the same girl their relations to'rds each other becomes strange. Here's the talk they spill:

"Where do you tend bar?" says Don.

"You got me guessed wrong," says Bill. "I work out to the Yards."

"Got anything on the hip?" says Don.

"You took the words out o' my mouth," says Bill. "I'm drier than St. Petersgrad."

"Stick round a w'ile and maybe we can scare up somethin'," says Don.

"I'll stick all right," says Bill. "They's a Jane in your party that's knocked me dead."

"What's her name?" says Don.

"Carmen," says Bill, Carmen bein' the girl's name in the show that Genevieve was takin' that part.

"Carmen!" says Joss. "Get offen that stuff! I and Carmen's just like two pavin' bricks."

"I should worry!" says Bill. "I ain't goin' to run away from no rat-eater."

"You're a rat-eater yourself, you rat-eater!" says Don.

"I'll rat-eat you!" says Bill.

And they go to it with a carvin' set, but they couldn't neither one o' them handle their utensils.

Don may of been all right slicin' toad-stools for the suey and Bill prob'ly could of massacreed a flock o' sheep with one stab, but they was all up in the air when it come to stickin' each other. They'd of did it better with dice.

Pretty soon the other actors can't stand it no longer and they come on yellin' "Fake!" So Don and Bill fold up their razors and Bill invites the whole bunch to come out and go through the Yards some mornin' and then he beats it, and the Michaels girl ain't did nothin' for fifteen minutes, so the management shoots her out for another song and she sings to Don about how he should ought to go home on account of his old lady bein' sick, so he asks Genevieve if she cares if he goes back to Janesville.

"Sure, I care," says Genevieve. "Go ahead!"

So the act winds up with everybody satisfied.

The last act's outside the Yards on the Halsted Street end. Bill's ast the entire company to come in and watch him croak a steer. The scene opens up with the crowd buyin' perfume and smellin' salts from the guys that's got the concessions. Pretty soon Eskimo Bill and Carmen drive in, all dressed up like a horse. Don's came in from Wisconsin and is hidin' in the bunch. He's sore at Carmen for not meetin' him on the Elevated platform.

He lays low till everybody's went inside, only Carmen. Then he braces her. He tells her his old lady's died and left him the laundry, and he wants her to go in with him and do the ironin'.

"Not me!" she says.

"What do you mean—'Not me'?" says Don.

"I and Bill's goin' to run a kosher market," she says.

24

Just about now you can hear noises behind the scenes like the cattle's gettin' theirs, so Carmen don't want to miss none of it, so she makes a break for the gate.

"Where you goin'?" says Joss.

"I want to see the butcherin'," she says.

"Stick round and I'll show you how it's done," says Joss.

So he pulls his knife and makes a pass at her, just foolin'. He misses her as far as from here to Des Moines. But she don't know he's kiddin' and she's scared to death. Yes, sir, she topples over as dead as the Federal League.

It was prob'ly her heart.

So now the whole crowd comes dashin' out because they's been a report that the place is infested with the hoof and mouth disease. They tell Don about it, but he's all excited over Carmen dyin'. He's delirious and gets himself mixed up with a Irish policeman.

"I yield me prisoner," he says.

Then the house doctor says the curtain's got

to come down to prevent the epidemic from spreadin' to the audience. So the show's over and the company's quarantined.

Well, Hatch was out all durin' the second act and part o' the third, and when he finally come back he didn't have to tell nobody where he'd been. And he dozed off the minute he hit his seat. I was for lettin' him sleep so's the rest o' the audience'd think we had one o' the op'ra bass singers in our party. But Mrs. Hatch wasn't lookin' for no publicity, on account of her costume, so she reached over and prodded him with a hatpin every time he begin a new aria.

Goin' out, I says to him:

"How'd you like it?"

"Pretty good," he says, "only they was too much gin in the last one."

"I mean the op'ra," I says.

"Don't ask him!" says Mrs. Hatch. "He didn't hear half of it and he didn't understand none of it."

"Oh, I wouldn't say that," says I. "Jim here ain't no boob, and they wasn't nothin' hard about it to understand."

"Not if you know the plot," says Mrs. Hatch.

"And somethin' about music," says my Missus.

"And got a little knowledge o' French," says Mrs. Hatch.

"Was that French they was singin'?" says Hatch. "I thought it was Wop or ostrich."

"That shows you up," says his Frau.

Well, when we got on the car for home they wasn't only one vacant seat and, o' course, Hatch had to have that. So I and my Missus and Mrs. Hatch clubbed together on the straps and I got a earful o' the real dope.

"What do you think o' Farr'r's costumes?" says Mrs. Hatch.

"Heavenly!" says my Missus. "Specially the one in the second act. It was all colors o' the rainbow."

"Hatch is right in style then," I says.

"And her actin' is perfect," says Mrs. Hatch.

"Her voice too," says the Wife.

"I liked her actin' better," says Mrs. H. "I thought her voice yodeled in the up-stairs registers."

"What do you suppose killed her?" I says.

"She was stabbed by her lover," says the Missus.

"You wasn't lookin'," I says. "He never touched her. It was prob'ly tobacco heart."

"He stabs her in the book," says Mrs. Hatch.

"It never went through the bindin'," I says.

"And wasn't Mooratory grand?" says the Wife.

"Splendid!" says Mrs. Hatch. "His actin' and singin' was both grand."

"I preferred his actin'," I says. "I thought his voice hissed in the down-stairs radiators."

This give them a good laugh, but they was soon at it again.

"And how sweet Alda was!" my Missus remarks.

"Which was her?" I ast them.

"The good girl," says Mrs. Hatch. "The girl that sung that beautiful aria in Atto Three."

"Atto girl!" I says. "I liked her too; the little Michaels girl. She came from Janesville."

"She did!" says Mrs. Hatch. "How do you know?"

So I thought I'd kid them along.

"My uncle told me," I says. "He used to be postmaster up there."

"What uncle was that?" says my wife.

"He ain't really my uncle," I says. "We all used to call him our uncle just like all these here singers calls the one o' them Daddy."

"They was a lady in back o' me," says Mrs. Hatch, "that says Daddy didn't appear tonight."

"Prob'ly the Missus' night out," I says.

"How'd you like the Tor'ador?" says Mrs. Hatch.

"I thought she moaned in the chimney," says I.

"It wasn't no 'she'," says the Missus. "We're talkin' about the bull-fighter."

"I didn't see no bull-fight," I says.

"It come off behind the scenes," says the Missus.

"When was you behind the scenes?" I says.

"I wasn't never," says my Missus. "But that's where it's supposed to come off."

"Well," I says, "you can take it from me that it wasn't pulled. Do you think the mayor'd stand for that stuff when he won't even leave them stage a box fight? You two girls has got a fine idear o' this here op'ra!"

"You know all about it, I guess," says the Missus. "You talk French so good!"

"I talk as much French as you do," I says. "But not nowheres near as much English, if you could call it that."

That kept her quiet, but Mrs. Hatch buzzed all the way home, and she was scared to death that the motorman wouldn't know where she'd been spendin' the evenin'. And if there was anybody in the car besides me that knowed *Car-*

men it must of been a joke to them hearin' her chatter. It wasn't no joke to me though. Hatch's berth was way off from us and they didn't nobody suspect him o' bein' in our party. I was standin' right up there with her where people couldn't help seein' that we was together.

I didn't want them to think she was my wife. So I kept smilin' at her. And when it finally come time to get off I hollered out loud at Hatch and says:

"All right, Hatch! Here's our street. Your Missus'll keep you awake the rest o' the way with her liberetto."

"It can't hurt no more than them hatpins," he says.

Well, when the paper come the next mornin' my Missus had to grab it up and turn right away to the place where the op'ras is wrote up. Under the article they was a list o' the ladies and gents in the boxes and what they wore, but it didn't say nothin' about what the gents wore, only the ladies. Prob'ly the ladies happened to have the most comical costumes that night, but I bet if the reporters could of saw Hatch they would of gave him a page to himself.

"Is your name there?" I says to the Missus.

"O' course not," she says. "They wasn't none o' them reporters tall enough to see us. You got to set in a box to be mentioned."

"Well," I says, "you don't care nothin' about bein' mentioned, do you?"

"O' course not," she says; but I could tell from how she said it that she wouldn't run down-town and horsewhip the editor if he made a mistake and printed about she and her costume; her costume wouldn't of et up all the space he had neither.

"How much does box seats cost?" I ast her.

"About six or seven dollars," she says.

"Well," I says, "let's I and you show Hatch up."

"What do you mean?" she says.

"I mean we should ought to return the compliment," says I. "We should ought to give them a party right back."

"We'd be broke for six weeks," she says.

"Oh, we'd do it with their money like they done it with ours," I says.

"Yes," she says; "but if you can ever win enough from the Hatches to buy four box seats to the op'ra I'd rather spend the money on a dress."

"Who said anything about four box seats?" I ast her.

"You did," she says.

"You're delirious!" I says. "Two box seats will be a plenty."

"Who's to set in them?" ast the Missus.

"Who do you think?" I says. "I and you is to set in them."

"But what about the Hatches?" she says.

"They'll set up where they was," says I. "Hatch picked out the seats before, and if he hadn't of wanted that altitude he'd of bought somewheres else."

"Yes," says the Missus, "but Mrs. Hatch won't think we're very polite to plant our guests in the Alps and we set down in a box."

"But they won't know where we're settin'," I says. "We'll tell them we couldn't get four seats together, so for them to set where they was the last time and we're goin' elsewheres."

"It don't seem fair," says my wife.

"I should worry about bein' fair with Hatch," I says. "If he's ever left with more than a dime's worth o' cards you got to look under the table for his hand."

"It don't seem fair," says the Missus.

"You should worry!" I says.

So we ast them over the followin' night and it looked for a minute like we was goin' to clean up. But after that one minute my Missus began collectin' pitcher cards again and every card Hatch drawed seemed like it was made to his measure. Well, sir, when we was through the lucky stiff was eight dollars to the good and Mrs. Hatch had about broke even.

"Do you suppose you can get them same seats?" I says.

"What seats?" says Hatch.

"For the op'ra," I says.

"You won't get me to no more op'ra," says Hatch. "I don't never go to the same show twicet."

"It ain't the same show, you goof!" I says. "They change the bill every day."

"They ain't goin' to change this eight-dollar bill o' mine," he says.

"You're a fine stiff!" I says.

"Call me anything you want to," says Hatch, "as long as you don't go over eight bucks' worth."

"Jim don't enjoy op'ra," says Mrs. Hatch.

"He don't enjoy nothin' that's more than a nickel," I says. "But as long as he's goin' to welsh on us I hope he lavishes the eight-spot where it'll do him some good."

"I'll do what I want to with it," says Hatch.

"Sure you will!" I says. "You'll bury it. But what you should ought to do is buy two suits o' clo'es."

So I went out in the kitchen and split a pint one way.

But don't think for a minute that I and the Missus ain't goin' to hear no more op'ra just because of a cheap stiff like him welshin'. I don't have to win in no rummy game before I spend.

We're goin' next Tuesday night, I and the Missus, and we're goin' to set somewheres near Congress Street. The show's *Armour's Do Re Mc*, a new one that's bein' gave for the first time. It's prob'ly named after some soap.

THREE KINGS AND A PAIR

Accordin' to some authorities, a person, before they get married, should ought to look up your opponent's family tree and find out what all her relatives died of. But the way I got it figured out, if you're sure they did die, the rest of it don't make no difference. In exceptionable cases it may be all right to take a girl that part of her family is still livin', but not under no circumstances if the part happens to be a unmarried sister named Bessie.

We was expectin' her in about two weeks, but we got a card Saturday mornin' which she says on it that she'd come right away if it was all the same to us, because it was the dull season in Wabash society and she could tear loose better at the present time than later on. Well, I guess they ain't no time in the year when society in Wabash would collapse for she not bein' there, but if she had to come at all, the sooner it was over the better. And besides, it wouldn't of did us no good to say aye, yes or no, because the postcard only beat her here by a few hours.

Not havin' no idear she was comin' so soon I didn't meet the train, but it seems like she brought her escort right along with her. It was a guy named Bishop and she'd met him on the trip up. The news butcher introduced them, I guess. He seen her safe to the house and she was there when I got home. Her and my Missus was full of him.

"Just think!" the Missus says. "He writes motion-pitcher plays."

"And gets ten thousand a year," says Bess.

"Did you find out from the firm?" I ast her.

"He told me himself," says Bessie.

"That's the right kind o' fella," says I, "open and above the board."

"Oh, you'll like Mr. Bishop," says Bess. "He says such funny things."

"Yes," I says, "that's a pretty good one about the ten thousand a year. But I suppose it's funnier when he tells it himself. I wisht I could meet him."

"They won't be no trouble about that," says the Missus. "He's comin' to dinner to-morrow and he's comin' to play cards some evenin' next week."

"What evenin'?" I says.

"Any evenin' that's convenient for you," says Bessie.

"Well," I says, "I'm sorry, but I got engagements every night except Monday, Wednesday, Thursday, Friday and Saturday."

"What about Tuesday?" ast Bessie.

"We're goin' to the op'ra," I says.

"Oh, won't that be grand!" says Bessie. "I wonder what I can wear."

"A kimono'll be all right," I says. "If the door-bell rings, you don't have to answer it."

"What do you mean?" says the Missus. "I guess if we go, Bess'll go with us."

"You'd starve to death if you guessed for a livin'," I says.

"Never mind that kind o' talk," says the Missus. "When we got a visitor we're not goin' out places nights and leave her here alone."

"What's the matter with Bishop?" I says. "They's lots o' two-handed card games."

"I ain't goin' to force myself on to you," says Bessie. "You don't have to take me nowheres if you don't want to."

"I wisht you'd put that in writin' in case of a lawsuit," I says.

"Listen here," says the Frau. "Get this straight: Either Bess goes or I don't go."

"You can both stay home," says I. "I don't anticipate no trouble findin' a partner."

"All right, that's settled," says the Missus. "We'll have a party of our own."

And it must of been goin' to be a dandy, because just speakin' about it made her cry. So I says:

"You win! But I'll prob'ly have to change the tickets."

40

"What kind o' tickets have you got?" ast the Missus.

"Cheap ones," I says. "Down-stairs, five per."

"How grand!" says Bessie.

"Yes," I says, "but I'm afraid I got the last two they had. I'll prob'ly have to give them back and take three balcony seats."

"That's all right, just so's Bess goes," says the Wife.

"Mr. Bishop's wild about music," says Bessie.

"Well," I says, "he prob'ly gets passes to the pitcher houses."

"He don't hear no real music there," says Bessie.

"Well," says I, "suppose when he comes to-morrow, I mention somethin' about I and the Missus havin' tickets to the op'ra Tuesday night. Then, if he's so wild about music, he'll maybe try to horn into the party and split the expenses fifty-fifty."

"That'd be a fine thing!" says the Frau. "He'd think we was a bunch o' cheap skates. Come right out and ask him to go at your expense, or else don't ask him at all."

"I won't ask him at all," I says. "It was a mistake for me to ever suggest it."

"Yes," says Bessie, "but after makin' the suggestion it would be a mean trick to not go through with it."

"Why?" I ast her. "He won't never know the difference."

"But I will," says Bessie.

"Course you would, dear," says the Missus. "After thinkin' you was goin' to have a man of your own, the party wouldn't seem like no party if you just went along with us."

"All right, all right," I says. "Let's not argue no more. Every time I open my head it costs three dollars."

"No such a thing," says the Missus. "The whole business won't only be two dollars more than you figured on. The tickets you had for the two of us would come to ten dollars, and with Bess and Mr. Bishop goin' it's only twelve, if you get balcony seats."

"I wonder," says Bessie, "if Mr. Bishop wouldn't object to settin' in the balcony."

"Maybe he would," says the Missus.

"Well," I says, "if he gets dizzy and falls over the railin' they's plenty of ushers to point out where he come from."

"They ain't no danger of him gettin' dizzy," says Bessie. "The only thing is that he's prob'ly used to settin' in the high-priced seats and would be embarrassed amongst the riff and raff."

"He can wear a false mustache for a disguise."

"He's got a real one," says Bessie.

"He can shave it off, then," says I.

"I wouldn't have him do that for the world," says Bessie. "It's too nice a one."

"You can't judge a mustache by seein' it oncet," I says. "It may be a crook at heart."

"This ain't gettin' us nowheres," says the Missus. "They's still a question before the house."

"It's up to Bess to give the answer," I says. "Bishop and his lip shield are invited if they'll set in a three-dollar seat."

"It's off, then," says Bessie, and beats it in the guest room and slams the door.

"What's the matter with you?" says the Missus.

"Nothin' at all," I says, "except that I ain't no millionaire scenario writer. Twenty dollars is twenty dollars."

"Yes," the Missus says, "but how many times have you lost more than that playin' cards and not thought nothin' of it?"

"That's different," I says. "When I spend money in a card game it's more like a investment. I got a chance to make somethin' by it."

"And this would be a investment, too," says the Wife, "and a whole lot better chance o' winnin' than in one o' them crooked card games."

"What are you gettin' at?" I ast her.

"This is what I'm gettin' at," she says, "though you'd ought to see it without me tellin' you. This here Bishop's made a big hit with Bess."

"It's been done before," says I.

"Listen to me," says the Frau. "It's high time she was gettin' married, and I don't want her marryin' none o' them Hoosier hicks."

"They'll see to that," I says. "They ain't such hicks."

"She could do a lot worse than take this here Bishop," the Missus says. "Ten thousand a year ain't no small change. And she'd be here in Chi; maybe they could find a flat right in this buildin'."

"That's all right," I says. "We could move."

"Don't be so smart," says the Missus. "It would be mighty nice for me to have her so near and it would be nice for you and I both to have a rich brother-in-law."

"I don't know about that," says I. "Somebody might do us a mischief in a fit o' jealous rage."

"He'd show us enough good times to make up for whatever they done," says the Wife. "We're foolish if we don't make no play for him and it'd be startin' off right to take him along to this here op'ra and set him in the best seats. He likes good music and you can see he's used to doin' things in style. And besides, sis looks her best when she's dressed up."

Well, I finally give in and the Missus called Bessie out o' the despondents' ward and they was all smiles and pep, but they acted like I wasn't in the house; so, to make it realistical, I blowed down to Andy's and looked after some o' my other investments.

We always have dinner Sundays at one o'clock, but o' course Bishop didn't know that and showed up prompt at ten bells, before I was half-way through the comical section. I had to go to the door because the Missus don't never put on her shoes till she's positive the family on the first floor is all awake, and Bessie was baskin' in the kind o' water that don't come in your lease at Wabash.

"Mr. Bishop, ain't it?" I says, lookin' him straight in the upper lip.

"How'd you know?" he says, smilin'.

"The girls told me to be expectin' a handsome man o' that name," I says. "And they told me about the mustache."

"Wouldn't be much to tell," says Bishop.

"It's young yet," I says. "Come in and take a weight off your feet."

So he picked out the only chair we got that ain't upholstered with flatirons and we set down and was tryin' to think o' somethin' more to say when Bessie hollered to us from mid-channel.

"Is that Mr. Bishop?" she yelped.

"It's me, Miss Gorton," says Bishop.

"I'll be right out," says Bess.

"Take it easy," I says. "You mightn't catch cold, but they's no use riskin' it."

So then I and Bishop knocked the street-car

service and President Wilson and give each other the double O. He wasn't what you could call ugly lookin', but if you'd come out in print and say he was handsome, a good lawyer'd have you at his mercy. His dimensions, what they was of them, all run perpendicular. He didn't have no latitude. If his collar slipped over his shoulders he could step out of it. If they hadn't been payin' him all them millions for pitcher plays, he could of got a job in a wire wheel. They wouldn't of been no difference in his photograph if you took it with a X-ray or a camera. But he had hair and two eyes and a mouth and all the rest of it, and his clo'es was certainly class. Why wouldn't they be? He could pick out cloth that was thirty bucks a yard and get a suit and overcoat for fifteen bucks. A umbrella cover would of made him a year's pyjamas.

Well, I seen the Missus sneak from the kitchen to her room to don the shoe leather, so I got right down to business.

48

"The girls tells me you're fond o' good music," I says.

"I love it," says Bishop.

"Do you ever take in the op'ra?" I ast him.

"I eat it up," he says.

"Have you been this year?" I says.

"Pretty near every night," says Bishop.

"I should think you'd be sick of it," says I.

"Oh, no," he says, "no more'n I get tired o' food."

"A man could easy get tired o' the same kind o' food," I says.

"But the op'ras is all different," says Bishop.

"Different languages, maybe," I says. "But they're all music and singin'."

"Yes," says Bishop, "but the music and singin' in the different op'ras is no more alike than lumbago and hives. They couldn't be nothin' differenter, for instance, than *Faust* and *Madame Buttermilk*."

"Unlest it was Scotch and chocolate soda," I says.

"They's good op'ras and bad op'ras," says Bishop.

"Which is the good ones?" I ast him.

"Oh," he says, *"Carmen* and *La Bohemian Girl* and *Ill Toreador."*

"Carmen's a bear cat," I says. "If they was all as good as *Carmen,* I'd go every night. But lots o' them is flivvers. They say they couldn't nothin' be worse than this *Armour's Dee Tree Ree."*

"It is pretty bad," says Bishop. "I seen it a year ago."

Well, I'd just been readin' in the paper where it was bran'-new and hadn't never been gave prev'ous to this season. So I thought I'd have a little sport with Mr. Smartenstein.

"What's it about?" I says.

He stalled a w'ile.

"It ain't about much of anything," he says.

"It must be about somethin'," says I.

"They got it all balled up the night I seen it," says Bishop. "The actors forgot their lines and a man couldn't make heads or tails of it."

"Did they sing in English?" I ast him.

"No; Latin," says Bishop.

"Can you understand Latin?" I says.

"Sure," says he. "I'd ought to. I studied it two years."

"What's the name of it mean in English?" I ast.

"You pronounce the Latin wrong," he says. "I can't parse it from how you say it. If I seen it wrote out I could tell."

So I handed him the paper where they give the op'ra schedule.

"That's her," I says, pointin' to the one that was billed for Tuesday night.

"Oh, yes," says Bishop. "Yes, that's the one."

"No question about that," says I. "But what does it mean?"

"I knowed you said it wrong," says Bishop. "The right pronouncement would be: *L. Armour's Day Trey Ray.* No wonder I was puzzled."

"Now the puzzle's solved," I says. "What

do them last three words mean? Louie Armour's what?"

"It ain't nothin' to do with Armour," says Bishop. "The first word is the Latin for love. And *Day* means of God, and *Trey* means three, and *Ray* means Kings."

"Oh," I says, "it's a poker game. The fella's just called and the other fella shows down his hand and the first fella had a straight and thought it wasn't no good. So he's su'prised to see what the other fella's got. So he says: 'Well, for the love o' Mike, three kings!' Only he makes it stronger. Is that the dope?"

"I don't think it's anything about poker," says Bishop.

"You'd ought to know," I says. "You seen it."

"But it was all jumbled up," says Bishop. "I couldn't get the plot."

"Do you suppose you could get it if you seen it again?" I says.

"I wouldn't set through it," he says. "It's no good."

Well, sir, I thought at the time that that little speech meant a savin' of eight dollars, because if he didn't go along, us three could set amongst the riff and raff. I dropped the subject right there and was goin' to tell the girls about it when he'd went home. But the Missus crabbed it a few minutes after her and Bess come in the room.

"Did you get your invitation?" says she to Bishop.

"What invitation?" he says.

"My husban' was goin' to ask you to go with us Tuesday night," she says. "Grand op'ra."

"Bishop won't go," I says. "He's already saw the play and says it ain't no good and he wouldn't feel like settin' through it again."

"Why, Mr. Bishop! That's a terrible disappointment," says the Missus.

"We was countin' on you," says Bessie, chokin' up.

"It's tough luck," I says, "but you can't expect things to break right all the w'ile."

"Wouldn't you change your mind?" says the Missus.

"That's up to your husban'," says Bishop. "I didn't understand that I was invited. I should certainly hate to break up a party, and if I'd knew I was goin' to be ast I would of spoke different about the op'ra. It's prob'ly a whole lot better than when I seen it. And, besides, I surely would enjoy your company."

"You can enjoy ourn most any night for nothin'," I says. "But if you don't enjoy the one down to the Auditorium, they's no use o' me payin' five iron men to have you bored to death."

"You got me wrong," says Bishop. "The piece was gave by a bunch o' supers the time I went. I'd like to see it with a real cast. They say it's a whiz when it's acted right."

"There!" says the Missus. "That settles it. You can change the tickets to-morrow."

So I was stopped and they wasn't no more to say, and after a w'ile we had dinner and then

I seen why Bishop was so skinny. 'Parently he hadn't tasted fodder before for a couple o' mont's.

"It must keep you busy writin' them scenarios," I says. "No time to eat or nothin'."

"Oh, I eat oncet in a w'ile even if I don't look it," he says. "I don't often get a chance at food that's cooked like this. Your wife's some dandy little cook!"

"It runs in the family, I guess," says Bessie. "You'd ought to taste my cookin'."

"Maybe he will some day," says the Missus, and then her and Bessie pretended like they'd made a break and was embarrassed.

So when he was through I says:

"Leave Bess take Bishop out in the kitchen and show him how she can wash dishes."

"Nothin' doin'," says the Wife. "I'm goin' to stack them and then I and you's got to hurry and keep our date."

"What date?" I says.

"Over to Hatch's," says the Missus. "You hadn't forgotten, had you?"

"I hadn't forgot that the Hatches was in Benton Harbor," I says.

"Yes," says the Frau, winkin' at me, "but I promised Mrs. Hatch I'd run over there and see that everything was O. K."

So I wasn't even allowed to set down and smoke, but had to help unload the table and then go out in the cold. And it was rotten weather and Sunday and nothin' but water, water everywhere.

"What's the idear?" I ast the Missus when we was out.

"Can't you see nothin'?" she says. "I want to give Bess a chance."

"Chance to what?" I says.

"A chance to talk to him," says the Wife.

"Oh!" says I. "I thought you wanted him to get stuck on her."

"What do you think of him?" says she. "Wouldn't he fit fine in the family?"

"He'd fit in a flute," I says. "He's the skinniest thing I ever seen. It seems like a shame to pay five dollars for a seat for him when him

56

and Bessie could sit in the same seat without contact."

"He is slender," says the Missus. "Prob'ly they been starvin' him where he boards at."

"I bet they wouldn't starve me on ten thousand a year," I says. "But maybe they don't know he's at the table or think he's just one o' the macaroni."

"It's all right for you to make jokes about him," says she, "but if you had his brains we'd be better off."

"If I had his brains," I says, "he'd go up like a balloon. If he lost an ounce, gravity wouldn't have no effect on him."

"You don't have to bulge out to be a man," says the Missus. "He's smart and he's rich and he's a swell dresser and I don't think we could find a better match for Bess."

"Match just describes him," says I.

"You're too cute to live," says the Wife. "But no matter what you say, him and Bess is goin' to hit it off. They're just suited to each other. They're a ideal pair."

"You win that argument," I says. "They're a pair all right, and they'd make a great hand if you was playin' deuces wild."

Well, we walked round till our feet was froze and then we went home, and Bishop says he would have to go, but the Missus ast him to stay to supper, and when he made the remark about havin' to go, he was referrin' to one o'clock the next mornin'. And right after supper I was gave the choice o' takin' another walk or hittin' the hay.

"Why don't we play cards?" I says.

"It's Sunday," says the Missus.

"Has the mayor stopped that, too?" I says.

But she winked at me again, the old flirt, so I stuck round the kitchen till it was pretty near time to wipe the dishes, and then I went to bed.

Monday noon I chased over to the Auditorium and they was only about eighty in line ahead o' me, and I was hopin' the house would be sold out for a week before I got up to the window. While I was markin' time I looked at the pitchers o' the different actors, hung up on the posts to advertise some kind o' hair tonic. I wisht I had Bishop along to tell me what the different names meant in English. I suppose most o' them meant Goatee or Spinach or Brush or Hedge or Thicket or somethin'. Then they was the girls' pitchers, too; Genevieve Farr'r that died in the Stockyards scene in *Carmen*, and Fanny Alda that took the part o' the Michaels girl from Janesville, and Mary Gardner, and Louise Edviney that was goin' to warble for us, and a lot more of all ages and one size.

Finally I got up to the ticket agent's cage and then I didn't only have to wait till the three women behind me done their shoppin', and then I hauled out my two tickets and ast the agent what would he give me for them.

"Do you want to exchange them?" he says.

"I did," says I, "but I heard you was sold out for to-morrow night."

"Oh, no," he says "we got plenty o' seats."

"But nothin' down-stairs, is they?" I says.

"Yes," he says "anywheres you want."

"Well," I says, "if you're sure you can spare them I want four in the place o' these two."

"Here's four nice ones in the seventh row," says he. "It'll be ten dollars more."

"I ain't partic'lar to have them nice," I says.

"It don't make no difference," says he. "The whole down-stairs is five a wallop."

"Yes," I says, "but one o' the four that's goin' is a little skinny fella and another's a refuge from Wabash."

"I don't care if they're all escapades from Milford Junction," he says. "We ain't runnin' no Hoosier Welfare League."

"You're smart, ain't you?" I says.

"I got to be," says the agent.

"But if you was a little smarter you'd be this side o' the cage instead o' that side," says I.

"Do you want these tickets or don't you?" he says.

So I seen he didn't care for no more verbal collisions with me, so I give him the two tickets and a bonus o' ten bucks and he give me back four pasteboards and throwed in a envelope free for nothin'.

I passed up lunch Tuesday because I wanted to get home early and have plenty o' time to dress. That was the idear and it worked out every bit as successful as the Peace Ship. In the first place, I couldn't get in my room because that's where the Missus and Bess was makin' up. In the second place, I didn't need to of allowed any time for supper because there wasn't none. The Wife said her and Bessie'd been so busy with their clo'es that they'd forgot a little thing like supper.

"But I didn't have no lunch," I says.

"That ain't my fault," says the Missus. "Besides, we can all go somewheres and eat after the show."

"On who?" I says.

"You're givin' the party," says she.

"The invitations didn't contain no clause about the inner man," says I. "Furthermore, if I had the ten dollars back that I spent to-

day for tickets, I'd have eleven dollars altogether."

"Well," says the Missus, "maybe Mr. Bishop
will have the hunch."

"He will if his hearin' 's good," says I.

Bishop showed up at six-thirty, lookin'
mighty cute in his waiter uniform. After he'd
came, it didn't take Bess long to finish her
toilet. I'd like to fell over when I seen her.
Some doll she was, too, in a fifty-meg evenin' dress marked down to thirty-seven. I
know, because I had helped pick it out for the
Missus.

"My, you look sweet!" says Bishop. "That's
a beautiful gown."

"It's my favoright," says Bessie.

"It don't take a person long to get attached
to a pretty dress," I says.

The Missus hollered for me to come in and
help her.

"I don't need no help," she says, "but I
didn't want you givin' no secrets away."

"What are you goin' to wear?" says I.

"Bess had one that just fits me," she says. "She's loanin' it to me."

"Her middle name's Generous," I says.

"Don't be sarcastical," says the Missus. "I want sis to look her best this oncet."

"And I suppose it don't make no difference how you look," says I, "as long as you only got me to please. If Bishop's friends sees him with Bessie they'll say: 'My! he's copped out a big-leaguer.' But if I run into any o' my pals they'll think I married the hired girl."

"You should worry," says the Missus.

"And besides that," I says, "if you succeed in tyin' Bishop up to a long-term lease he's bound to see that there dress on you some time and then what'll he think?"

"Bess can keep the gown," says the Missus. "I'll make her give me one of her'n for it."

"With your tradin' ability," I says, "you'd ought to be the Cincinnati Reds' manager. But if you do give the dress to her," I says, "warn her not to wear it in Wabash—except when the marshal's over on the other street."

Well, we was ready in a few minutes, because I'm gettin' used to the soup and fish, and everything went on easy owin' to my vacuum, and I was too weak to shave; and the Missus didn't have no trouble with Bessie's creation, which was built like the Cottage Grove cars, enter at front.

"I don't think I'm so bad," says the Missus, lookin' in the glass.

"You'd be just right," I says, "if we was goin' to the annual meetin' o' the Woman's Guild."

I and Bishop had a race gettin' on the streetcar. I was first and he won.

"I just got paid to-day," he says, "and I didn't have time to get change."

They wasn't only one seat. Bess took it first and then offered it to the Missus.

"I'll be mad at you if you don't take it," says Bess.

But the wife remained standin' and Bessie by a great effort kept her temper.

Goin' into the theayter we passed a fella that was sellin' liberettos.

"I bet this guy's got lots o' change," I says.

"Them things is for people that ain't never saw no op'ra," says Bishop.

"I'm goin' to have one," I says.

"Don't buy none for me," says Bishop.

"You just spoke in time," I says.

I laid down a quarter and grabbed one o' the books.

"It's thirty-five cents," says the guy.

"*Carmen* wasn't only a quarter," I says. "Is this show better'n *Carmen?*"

"This is a new one," the guy says.

"This fella," I says, pointin' to Bishop, "seen it a year ago."

"He must have a good imagination," says the guy.

"No," I says, "he writes movin'-pitcher plays."

I give up a extra dime, because they didn't seem to be nothin' else to do. Then I handed over my tickets to the fella at the door and we

was took right down amongst the high polloi.
Say, I thought the dress Bess was wearin' was
low; ought to been, seein' it was cut down from
fifty bucks to thirty-seven. But the rest o' the
gowns round us must of been sixty per cent.
off.

I says to the Missus:

"I bet you wisht now you hadn't swapped
costumes."

"Oh, I don't know," she says. "It's chilly
in here."

Well, it may of been chilly then, but not
after the op'ra got goin' good. Carmen was
a human refrigerator compared to the leadin'
lady in this show. Set through two acts and
you couldn't hardly believe it was December.

But the curtain was supposed to go up at
eight-ten, and it wasn't only about that time
when we got there, so they was over half a hour
to kill before the show begin. I looked in my
program and seen the real translation o' the
title. *The Love o' Three Kings,* it says, and

no "of God" to it. I'd of knew anyway, when I'd read the plot, that He didn't have nothin' to do with it.

I listened a w'ile to Bishop and Bess.

"And you've saw all the op'ras?" she ast him.

"Most o' them," he says.

"How grand!" says Bessie. "I wisht I could see a lot o' them."

"Well," he says, "you're goin' to be here for some time."

"Oh, Mr. Bishop, I don't want you throwin' all your money away on me," she says.

"I don't call it throwin' money away," says Bishop.

"I wouldn't neither," I says. "I'd say Bishop was muscle-bound."

They didn't pay no attention to me.

"What ones would you like to see?" he ast her.

"What are your favorights?" says Bess.

"Oh," says Bishop, "I've saw them all so many times that it don't really make no difference to me. Sometimes they give two the same night, two short ones, and then you ain't so liable to get bored."

Saturday nights is when they usually give the two, and Saturday nights they cut the prices. This here Bishop wasn't no boob.

"One good combination," he says, "is *Polly Archer* and *Cavalier Rusticana*. They're both awful pretty."

"Oh, I'd love to see them," says Bessie. "What are they like?"

So he says Polly Archer was a leadin' lady in a stock company and the leadin' man and another fella was both stuck on her and she loved one o' them—I forget which one; whichever wasn't her husbun'—and they was a place in one o' their shows where the one that was her husbun' was supposed to get jealous and stab she and her lover, just actin', but, instead o' just pretendin', this one night he played a joke on them and done the stabbin' in earnest, and they was both killed. Well, that'd be a good one to see if you happened to be there the night he really kills them; otherwise, it sounds pretty tame. And Bishop also told her about *Cavalier Rusticana* that means Rural Free Delivery in English, and I didn't get the plot only that the mail carrier flirts with one o' the farmers' wives and o' course the rube spears him with a pitchfork. The state's attorneys must of been on the jump all the w'ile in them days.

Finally the orchestra was all in their places and an old guy with a beard come out in front o' them.

"That's the conductor," says Bishop.

"He looks like he'd been a long time with the road," I says.

Then up went the curtain and the thermometer.

The scene's laid in Little Italy, but you can't see nothin' when it starts off because it's supposed to be just before mornin'. Pretty soon one o' the three kings comes in with a grouch. He's old and blind as a bat and he ain't slept good and he's sore at the conductor on account o' the train bein' a half-hour late, and the conductor's jealous of him because his beard's longer, and Archibald, that's the old king's name, won't sing what the orchestra's playin', but just snarls and growls, and the orchestra can't locate what key he's snarlin' in, so they don't get along at all, and finally Flamingo, that's the old king's chauffeur, steers him off'n the stage.

Acrost on the other side o' the stage from where they go off they's a bungalow, and out of it comes Flora and another o' the kings, a young fella with a tenor voice named Veto. They sing about what a fine mornin' it is in Wop and she tells him he'd better fly his kite before Archibald catches him.

It seems like she's married to Archibald's son, Fred, but o' course she likes Veto better or it wouldn't be no op'ra. Her and Veto was raised in the same ward and they was oncet engaged to be married, but Archibald's gang trimmed Veto's in a big roughhouse one night and Flora was part o' the spoils. When Archibald seen how good she could fix spaghett' he was bound she'd stick in the family, so he give her the choice o' bein' killed or marryin' his boy, so she took Fred but didn't really mean it in earnest. So Veto hangs round the house a lot, because old Archibald's blind and Fred's generally always on the road with the Erie section gang.

But old Archibald's eyes bein' no good, his ears is so much the better, even if he don't sometimes keep with the orchestra, so he comes back on the stage just after Veto's went and he hears Flora tryin' to snoop back in her bungalow.

"Who was you talkin' to?" he says.

"Myself," says Flora.

"Great stuff!" says Archibald. "Up and outdoors at five A. M. to talk to yourself! Feed that to the goldfish!"

So she ain't got him fooled for a minute, but w'ile they're arguin' Fred blows in. So Archibald don't say nothin' about his superstition because he ain't sure, so Fred and his Missus goes in the bungalow to have breakfast and Archibald stays on the stage quarrelin' with the conductor.

If Fred was eatin' all through the intermission, he must of been as hungry as me, because it was plain forty minutes before the second act begin. Him and Flora comes out o' their house and Fred says he's got to go right away again because they's a bad wash-out this side o' Huntington. He ain't no sooner gone than Veto's back on the job, but Flora's kind o' sorry for her husbun', and Veto don't get the reception that a star ought to expect.

"Why don't you smile at me?" he says.

So she says:

"It don't seem proper, dearie, with a husbun' on the Erie."

But before long she can't resist his high notes and the next five or ten minutes is a love scene between the two, and they was a couple o' times when I thought the management would ring down the asbestos curtain. Finally old Archibald snoops back on the stage with Flamingo, and Veto runs, but Archie hears him and it's good night. The old boy gives Flora the third degree and she owns up, and then Flamingo says that Fred's comin' back to get his dinner pail. So Archibald insists on knowin' the fella's name that he heard him runnin' away, but Flora's either forgot it or else she's stubborn, so Archie looses his temper and wrings her neck. So when Fred arrives he gets the su'prise of his life and finds out he's a widow.

"I slayed her," says Archibald. "She wasn't no good."

"She was the best cook we ever had," says Fred. "What was the matter with her?"

"She had a gentleman friend," says his old man.

Well, so far, they's only one dead and nothin' original about how it was pulled. You can go over to the Victoria and see any number o' throttlin's at fifty cents for the best seats. So it was up to the management to get a wallop into the last act. It took them pretty near forty minutes to think of it, but it was good when it come.

The scene is Colosimo's undertakin' rooms and Flora's ruins is laid out on the counter. All the Wops from her ward stand round singin' gospel hymns.

When they've beat it Veto approaches the bier bar and wastes some pretty fair singin' on the late Flora. Then all of a sudden he leans over and gives her a kiss. That's all for Veto. You see, Old Fox Archibald had figured that the bird that loved her would pull somethin' like this and he'd doped out a way to learn who he was and make him regret it at the same time, besides springin' some bran'-new stuff in the killin' line. So he's mixed up some rat poison and garlic and spread it on the lips of his fair daughter-in-law.

W'ile Veto's dyin' Fred comes in and finds him.

"So it was you, was it?" he says.

"I'm the guy," says Veto.

"Well," says Fred, "this'll learn you a lesson, you old masher, you!"

"I'll mash you in a minute," says Veto, but

the way he was now, he couldn't of mashed turnips.

"I kissed her last, anyway," says Veto.

"You think you did!" says Fred, and helps himself to the garlic.

So Veto's dead and Fred's leanin' over the counter, dyin', when Archibald wabbles in. He finds his way up to Fred and grabs a hold of him, thinkin' it's the stranger.

"Lay off'n me, pa," says Fred. "This ain't the other bird. He's dead and it's got me, too."

"Well," says the old man, "that'd ought to satisfy them. But it's pretty tough on the Erie."

"How grand!" says Bess when it was over.

"But it leaves you with a bad taste," says Bishop.

"And a big appetite," I says.

"Did that old man kill them all?" ast the Missus.

"All but hisself and Flamingo," says I.

"What was he mad at?" says she.

"He was drove crazy by hunger," I says. "His wife and his sister-in-law and her fella was starvin' him to death."

"Bein' blind, he prob'ly spilled things at table," says the Missus. "Blind men sometimes has trouble gettin' their food."

"The trouble ain't confined to the blind," says I.

When we got outside I left Bess and Bishop lead the way, hopin' they'd head to'rds a steak garage.

"No hurry about gettin' home," I hollered to them. "The night's still young yet."

Bishop turned round.

"Is they any good eatin' places out by your place?" he says.

I thought I had him.

"Not as good as down-town," says I, and I named the Loop restaurants.

"How's the car service after midnight?" he says.

"Grand!" says I. "All night long."

THREE KINGS AND A PAIR

I wondered where he would take us. Him and Bess crossed the avenue and stopped where the crowd was waitin' for south-bound cars.

"He's got some favorite place a ways south," says the Missus.

A car come and I and her clumb aboard. We looked back just in time to see Bessie and Bishop wavin' us farewell.

"They missed the car," says the Missus.

"Yes," I says, "and they was just as anxious to catch it as if it'd been the leprosy."

"Never mind," says the Missus. "If he wants to be alone with her it's a good sign."

"I can't eat a sign," says I.

"We'll stop at The Ideal and have a little supper of our own," she says.

"We won't," says I.

"Why not?" says the Missus.

"Because," I says, "they's exactly thirty-five cents in my pocket. And offerin' my stomach seventeen and a half cents' worth o' food now would be just about like sendin' one blank cartridge to the Russian army."

77

"I think they's some crackers in the house," she says.

"Prob'ly," says I. "We're usually that way —overstocked. You don't seem to realize that our household goods is only insured for a thousand."

About one o'clock I went to sleep from sheer weakness. About one-thirty the Missus shook me and woke me up.

"We win, Joe!" she says, all excited. "I think Bishop and Bess is engaged!"

"Win!" says I. "Say, if you was a Frenchman you'd have a big celebration every anniversary o' the Battle o' Waterloo."

"I was goin' out in the kitchen to get a drink," she says. "Bess was home, but I didn't know it. And when I was comin' back from the kitchen I happened to glance in the livin'-room. And I seen Bishop kiss her! Isn't it great!"

"Yes," I says. "But I wisht she'd of had Archibald fix up her lips."

GULLIBLE'S TRAVELS

I

I PROMISED the Wife that if anybody ast me what kind of a time did I have at Palm Beach I'd say I had a swell time. And if they ast me who did we meet I'd tell 'em everybody that was worth meetin'. And if they ast me didn't the trip cost a lot I'd say Yes; but it was worth the money. I promised her I wouldn't spill none o' the real details. But if you can't break a promise you made to your own wife what kind of a promise can you break? Answer me that, Edgar.

I'm not one o' these kind o' people that'd keep a joke to themself just because the joke was on them. But they's plenty of our friends that I wouldn't have 'em hear about it for the world. I wouldn't tell you, only I know you're not the village gossip and won't crack it to anybody. Not even to your own Missus, see? I don't trust no women.

It was along last January when I and the Wife was both hit by the society bacillus. I think it was at the opera. You remember me tellin' you about us and the Hatches goin' to *Carmen* and then me takin' my Missus and her sister, Bess, and four of one suit named Bishop to see *The Three Kings?* Well, I'll own up that I enjoyed wearin' the soup and fish and minglin' amongst the high polloi and pretendin' we really was somebody. And I know my wife enjoyed it, too, though they was nothin' said between us at the time.

The next stage was where our friends wasn't good enough for us no more. We used to be tickled to death to spend an evenin' playin' rummy with the Hatches. But all of a sudden they didn't seem to be no fun in it and when Hatch'd call up we'd stall out of it. From the number o' times I told him that I or the Missus was tired out and goin' right to bed, he must of thought we'd got jobs as telephone linemen.

We quit attendin' pitcher shows because the

rest o' the audience wasn't the kind o' people you'd care to mix with. We didn't go over to Ben's and dance because they wasn't no class to the crowd there. About once a week we'd beat it to one o' the good hotels down-town, all dressed up like a horse, and have our dinner with the rest o' the E-light. They wasn't nobody talked to us only the waiters, but we could look as much as we liked and it was sport tryin' to guess the names o' the gang at the next table.

Then we took to readin' the society news at breakfast. It used to be that I didn't waste time on nothin' but the market and sportin' pages, but now I pass 'em up and listen w'ile the Missus rattled off what was doin' on the Lake Shore Drive.

Every little w'ile we'd see where So-and-So was at Palm Beach or just goin' there or just comin' back. We got to kiddin' about it.

"Well," I'd say, "we'd better be startin' pretty soon or we'll miss the best part o' the season."

"Yes," the Wife'd say back, "we'd go right now if it wasn't for all them engagements next week."

We kidded and kidded till finally, one night, she forgot we was just kiddin'.

"You didn't take no vacation last summer," she says.

"No," says I. "They wasn't no chance to get away."

"But you promised me," she says, "that you'd take one this winter to make up for it."

"I know I did," I says; "but it'd be a sucker play to take a vacation in weather like this."

"The weather ain't like this everywheres," she says.

"You must of been goin' to night school," I says.

"Another thing you promised me," says she, "was that when you could afford it you'd take me on a real honeymoon trip to make up for the dinky one we had."

"That still goes," I says, "when I can afford it."

"You can afford it now," says she. "We don't owe nothin' and we got money in the bank."

"Yes," I says. "Pretty close to three hundred bucks."

"You forgot somethin'," she says. "You forgot them war babies."

Did I tell you about that? Last fall I done a little dabblin' in Crucial Steel and at this time I'm tellin' you about I still had a hold of it, but stood to pull down six hundred. Not bad, eh?

"It'd be a mistake to let loose now," I says.

"All right," she says. "Hold on, and I hope you lose every cent. You never did care nothin' for me."

Then we done a little spoonin' and then I ast her what was the big idear.

"We ain't swelled on ourself," she says; "but I know and you know that the friends we been associatin' with ain't in our class. They don't know how to dress and they can't talk about nothin' but their goldfish and their meat bills.

They don't try to get nowheres, but all they do is play rummy and take in the Majestic. I and you like nice people and good music and things that's worth w'ile. It's a crime for us to be wastin' our time with riff and raff that'd run round barefooted if it wasn't for the police."

"I wouldn't say we'd wasted much time on 'em lately," I says.

"No," says she, "and I've had a better time these last three weeks than I ever had in my life."

"And you can keep right on havin' it," I says.

"I could have a whole lot better time, and you could, too," she says, "if we could get acquainted with some congenial people to go round with; people that's tastes is the same as ourn."

"If any o' them people calls up on the phone," I says, "I'll be as pleasant to 'em as I can."

"You're always too smart," says the Wife.

"You don't never pay attention to no schemes o' mine."

"What's the scheme now?"

"You'll find fault with it because I thought it up," she says. "If it was your scheme you'd think it was grand."

"If it really was good you wouldn't be scared to spring it," I says.

"Will you promise to go through with it?" says she.

"If it ain't too ridic'lous," I told her.

"See! I knowed that'd be the way," she says.

"Don't talk crazy," I says. "Where'd we be if we'd went through with every plan you ever sprang?"

"Will you promise to listen to my side of it without actin' cute?" she says.

So I didn't see no harm in goin' that far.

"I want you to take me to Palm Beach," says she. "I want you to take a vacation, and that's where we'll spend it."

"And that ain't all we'd spend," I says.

"Remember your promise," says she.

So I shut up and listened.

The dope she give me was along these lines: We could get special round-trip rates on any o' the railroads and that part of it wouldn't cost nowheres near as much as a man'd naturally think. The hotel rates was pretty steep, but the meals was throwed in, and just imagine what them meals would be! And we'd be stayin' under the same roof with the Vanderbilts and Goulds, and eatin' at the same table, and probably, before we was there a week, callin' 'em Steve and Gus. They was dancin' every night and all the guests danced with each other, and how would it feel fox-trottin' with the president o' the B. & O., or the Delmonico girls from New York! And all Chicago society was down there, and when we met 'em we'd know 'em for life and have some real friends amongst 'em when we got back home.

That's how she had it figured and she must of been practisin' her speech, because it certainly did sound good to me. To make it short, I fell, and dated her up to meet me down-town

the next day and call on the railroad bandits.
The first one we seen admitted that his was
the best route and that he wouldn't only soak
us one hundred and forty-seven dollars and
seventy cents to and from Palm Beach and
back, includin' an apartment from here to
Jacksonville and as many stop-overs as we
wanted to make. He told us we wouldn't have
to write for no hotel accommodations because
the hotels had an agent right over on Madison
Street that'd be glad to do everything to us.

So we says we'd be back later and then we
beat it over to the Florida East Coast's local
studio.

"How much for a double room by the week?"
I ast the man.

"They ain't no weekly rates," he says. "By
the day it'd be twelve dollars and up for two
at the Breakers, and fourteen dollars and up
at the Poinciana."

"I like the Breakers better," says I.

"You can't get in there," he says. "They're
full for the season."

"That's a long spree," I says.

"Can we get in the other hotel?" ast the Wife.

"I can find out," says the man.

"We want a room with bath," says she.

"That'd be more," says he. "That'd be fifteen dollars or sixteen dollars and up."

"What do we want of a bath," I says, "with the whole Atlantic Ocean in the front yard?"

"I'm afraid you'd have trouble gettin' a bath," says the man. "The hotels is both o' them pretty well filled up on account o' the war in Europe."

"What's that got to do with it?" I ast him.

"A whole lot," he says. "The people that usually goes abroad is all down to Palm Beach this winter."

"I don't see why," I says. "If one o' them U-boats hit 'em they'd at least be gettin' their bath for nothin'."

We left him with the understandin' that he was to wire down there and find out what was the best they could give us. We called him up in a couple o' days and he told us we could

have a double room, without no bath, at the
Poinciana, beginnin' the fifteenth o' February.
He didn't know just what the price would be.

Well, I fixed it up to take my vacation startin' the tenth, and sold out my Crucial Steel,
and divided the spoils with the railroad company. We decided we'd stop off in St. Augustine two days, because the Missus found out
somewheres that they might be two or three
o' the Four Hundred lingerin' there, and we
didn't want to miss nobody.

"Now," I says, "all we got to do is set round
and wait for the tenth o' the month."

"Is that so!" says the Wife. "I suppose
you're perfectly satisfied with your clo'es."

"I've got to be," I says, "unless the Salvation
Army has somethin' that'll fit me."

"What's the matter with our charge account?" she says.

"I don't like to charge nothin'," I says,
"when I know they ain't no chance of ever
payin' for it."

"All right," she says, "then we're not goin'

to Palm Beach. I'd rather stay home than go down there lookin' like general housework."

"Do you need clo'es yourself?" I ast her.

"I certainly do," she says. "About two hundred dollars' worth. But I got one hundred and fifty dollars o' my own."

"All right," I says. "I'll stand for the other fifty and then we're all set."

"No, we're not," she says. "That just fixes me. But I want you to look as good as I do."

"Nature'll see to that," I says.

But they was no arguin' with her. Our trip, she says, was an investment; it was goin' to get us in right with people worth w'ile. And we wouldn't have a chance in the world unless we looked the part.

So before the tenth come round, we was long two new evenin' gowns, two female sport suits, four or five pairs o' shoes, all colors, one Tuxedo dinner coat, three dress shirts, half a dozen other kinds o' shirts, two pairs o' transparent white trousers, one new business suit and Lord knows how much underwear and how many hats and stockin's. And I had till the fifteenth o' March to pay off the mortgage on the old homestead.

Just as we was gettin' ready to leave for the train the phone rung. It was Mrs. Hatch and she wanted us to come over for a little rummy. I was shavin' and the Missus done the talkin'.

"What did you tell her?" I ast.

"I told her we was goin' away," says the Wife.

"I bet you forgot to mention where we was goin'," I says.

"Pay me," says she.

II

I thought we was in Venice when we woke up next mornin', but the porter says it was just Cairo, Illinois. The river'd went crazy and I bet they wasn't a room without a bath in that old burg.

As we set down in the diner for breakfast the train was goin' acrost the longest bridge

I ever seen, and it looked like we was so near the water that you could reach right out and grab a handful. The Wife was a little wabbly.

"I wonder if it's really safe," she says.

"If the bridge stays up we're all right," says I.

"But the question is, Will it stay up?" she says.

"I wouldn't bet a nickel either way on a bridge," I says. "They're treacherous little devils. They'd cross you as quick as they'd cross this river."

"The trainmen must be nervous," she says. "Just see how we're draggin' along."

"They're givin' the fish a chance to get offen the track," I says. "It's against the law to spear fish with a cowcatcher this time o' year."

Well, the Wife was so nervous she couldn't eat nothin' but toast and coffee, so I figured I was justified in goin' to the prunes and steak and eggs.

After breakfast we went out in what they call the sun parlor. It was a glassed-in room on the tail-end o' the rear coach and it must of been a pleasant place to set and watch the scenery. But they was a gang o' missionaries or somethin' had all the seats and they never budged out o' them all day. Every time they'd come to a crossroads they'd toss a stack o' Bible studies out o' the back window for the southern heathen to pick up and read. I suppose they thought they was doin' a lot o' good for their fellow men, but their fellow passengers meanw'ile was gettin' the worst of it.

Speakin' o' the scenery, it certainly was somethin' grand. First we'd pass a few pine trees with fuzz on 'em and then a couple o' acres o' yellow mud. Then they'd be more pine trees and more fuzz and then more yellow mud. And after a w'ile we'd come to some pine trees with fuzz on 'em and then, if we watched close, we'd see some yellow mud.

Every few minutes the train'd stop and then start up again on low. That meant the engineer suspected he was comin' to a station and was scared that if he run too fast he wouldn't

see it, and if he run past it without stoppin'
the inhabitants wouldn't never forgive him.
You see, they's a regular schedule o' duties
that's followed out by the more prominent citi-
zens down those parts. After their wife's at-
tended to the chores and got the breakfast they
roll out o' bed and put on their overalls and
eat. Then they get on their horse or mule or
cow or dog and ride down to the station and
wait for the next train. When it comes they
have a contest to see which can count the passengers first. The losers has to promise to
work one day the followin' month. If one fella
loses three times in the same month he generally always kills himself.

All the towns has got five or six private res-
idences and seven or eight two-apartment
buildin's and a grocery and a post-office. They
told me that somebody in one o' them burgs,
I forget which one, got a letter the day before
we come through. It was misdirected, I guess.

The two-apartment buildin's is constructed
on the ground floor, with a porch to divide one

flat from the other. One's the housekeepin' side and the other's just a place for the husband and father to lay round in so's they won't be disturbed by watchin' the women work.

It was a blessin' to them boys when their states went dry. Just think what a strain it must of been to keep liftin' glasses and huntin' in their overalls for a dime!

In the afternoon the Missus went into our apartment and took a nap and I moseyed into the readin'-room and looked over some o' the comical magazines. They was a fat guy come in and set next to me. I'd heard him, in at lunch, tellin' the dinin'-car conductor what Wilson should of done, so I wasn't su'prised when he opened up on me.

"Tiresome trip," he says.

I didn't think it was worth w'ile arguin' with him.

"Must of been a lot o' rain through here," he says.

"Either that," says I, "or else the sprinklin' wagon run shy o' streets."

He laughed as much as it was worth.

"Where do you come from?" he ast me.

"Dear old Chicago," I says.

"I'm from St. Louis," he says.

"You're frank," says I.

"I'm really as much at home one place as another," he says. "The Wife likes to travel and why shouldn't I humor her?"

"I don't know," I says. "I haven't the pleasure."

"Seems like we're goin' all the w'ile," says he. "It's Hot Springs or New Orleans or Florida or Atlantic City or California or somewheres."

"Do you get passes?" I ast him.

"I guess I could if I wanted to," he says. "Some o' my best friends is way up in the railroad business."

"I got one like that," I says. "He generally stands on the fourth or fifth car behind the engine."

"Do you travel much?" he ast me.

"I don't live in St. Louis," says I.

"Is this your first trip south?" he ast.

"Oh, no," I says. "I live on Sixty-fifth Street."

"I meant, have you ever been down this way before?"

"Oh, yes," says I. "I come down every winter."

"Where do you go?" he ast.

That's what I was layin' for.

"Palm Beach," says I.

"I used to go there," he says. "But I've cut it out. It ain't like it used to be. They leave everybody in now."

"Yes," I says; "but a man don't have to mix up with 'em."

"You can't just ignore people that comes up and talks to you," he says.

"Are you bothered that way much?" I ast.

"It's what drove me away from Palm Beach," he says.

"How long since you been there?" I ast him.

"How long you been goin' there?" he says.

"Me?" says I. "Five years."

"We just missed each other," says he. "I quit six years ago this winter."

"Then it couldn't of been there I seen you," says I. "But I know I seen you somewheres before."

"It might of been most anywheres," he says. "They's few places I haven't been at."

"Maybe it was acrost the pond," says I.

"Very likely," he says. "But not since the war started. I been steerin' clear of Europe for two years."

"So have I, for longer'n that," I says.

"It's certainly an awful thing, this war," says he.

"I believe you're right," says I; "but I haven't heard nobody express it just that way before."

"I only hope," he says, "that we succeed in keepin' out of it."

"If we got in, would you go?" I ast him.

"Yes, sir," he says.

"You wouldn't beat me," says I. "I bet I'd reach Brazil as quick as you."

"Oh, I don't think they'd be any action in South America," he says. "We'd fight defensive at first and most of it would be along the Atlantic Coast."

"Then maybe we could get accommodations in Yellowstone Park," says I.

"They's no sense in this country gettin' involved," he says. "Wilson hasn't handled it right. He either ought to of went stronger or not so strong. He's wrote too many notes."

"You certainly get right to the root of a thing," says I. "You must of thought a good deal about it."

"I know the conditions pretty well," he says. "I know how far you can go with them people over there. I been amongst 'em a good part o' the time."

"I suppose," says I, "that a fella just naturally don't like to butt in. But if I was you I'd consider it my duty to romp down to Washington and give 'em all the information I had."

"Wilson picked his own advisers," says he. "Let him learn his lesson."

"That ain't hardly fair," I says. "Maybe you was out o' town, or your phone was busy or somethin'."

"I don't know Wilson nor he don't know me," he says.

"That oughtn't to stop you from helpin' him out," says I. "If you seen a man drownin' would you wait for some friend o' the both o' you to come along and make the introduction?"

"They ain't no comparison in them two cases," he says. "Wilson ain't never called on me for help."

"You don't know if he has or not," I says. "You don't stick in one place long enough for a man to reach you."

"My office in St. Louis always knows where I'm at," says he. "My stenographer can reach me any time within ten to twelve hours."

"I don't think it's right to have this country's whole future dependin' on a St. Louis stenographer," I says.

"That's nonsense!" says he. "I ain't makin' no claim that I could save or not save this country. But if I and Wilson was acquainted I might tell him some facts that'd help him out in his foreign policy."

"Well, then," I says, "it's up to you to get acquainted. I'd introduce you myself only I don't know your name."

"My name's Gould," says he; "but you're not acquainted with Wilson."

"I could be, easy," says I. "I could get on a train he was goin' somewheres on and then go and set beside him and begin to talk. Lots o' people make friends that way."

It was gettin' along to'rd supper-time, so I excused myself and went back to the apartment. The Missus had woke up and wasn't feelin' good.

"What's the matter?" I ast her.

"This old train," she says. "I'll die if it don't stop goin' round them curves."

"As long as the track curves, the best thing the train can do is curve with it," I says. "You may die if it keeps curvin', but you'd die a whole lot sooner if it left the rails and went straight ahead."

"What you been doin'?" she ast me.

"Just talkin' to one o' the Goulds," I says.

"Gould!" she says. "What Gould?"

"Well," I says, "I didn't ask him his first name, but he's from St. Louis, so I suppose it's Ludwig or Heinie."

"Oh," she says, disgusted. "I thought you meant one o' the real ones."

"He's a real one, all right," says I. "He's so classy that he's passed up Palm Beach. He says it's gettin' too common."

"I don't believe it," says the Wife. "And besides, we don't have to mix up with everybody."

"He says they butt right in on you," I told her.

"They'll get a cold reception from me," she says.

But between the curves and the fear o' Palm Beach not bein' so exclusive as it used to be, she couldn't eat no supper, and I had another big meal.

The next mornin' we landed in Jacksonville three hours behind time and narrowly missed connections for St. Augustine by over an hour and a half. They wasn't another train till one-thirty in the afternoon, so we had some time to kill. I went shoppin' and bought a shave and five or six rickeys. The Wife helped herself to a chair in the writin'-room of one o' the hotels and told pretty near everybody in Chicago that she wished they was along with us, accompanied by a pitcher o' the Elks' Home or the Germania Club, or Trout Fishin' at Atlantic Beach.

W'ile I was gettin' my dime's worth in the tonsorial parlors, I happened to look up at a calendar on the wall, and noticed it was the twelfth o' February.

"How does it come that everything's open here to-day?" I says to the barber. "Don't you-all know it's Lincoln's birthday?"

"Is that so?" he says. "How old is he?"

III

We'd wired ahead for rooms at the Alcazar, and when we landed in St. Augustine they was a motor-bus from the hotel to meet us at the station.

"Southern hospitality," I says to the Wife, and we was both pleased till they relieved us o' four bits apiece for the ride.

Well, they hadn't neither one of us slept good the night before, w'ile we was joltin' through Georgia; so when I suggested a nap they wasn't no argument.

"But our clo'es ought to be pressed," says the Missus. "Call up the valet and have it done w'ile we sleep."

So I called up the valet, and sure enough, he come.

"Hello, George!" I says. "You see, we're goin' to lay down and take a nap, and we was wonderin' if you could crease up these two suits and have 'em back here by the time we want 'em."

"Certainly, sir," says he.

"And how much will it cost?" I ast him.

"One dollar a suit," he says.

"Are you on parole or haven't you never been caught?" says I.

"Yes, sir," he says, and smiled like it was a joke.

"Let's talk business, George," I says. "The tailor we go to on Sixty-third walks two blocks to get our clo'es, and two blocks to take 'em to his joint, and two blocks to bring 'em back, and he only soaks us thirty-five cents a suit."

"He gets poor pay and he does poor work," says the burglar. "When I press clo'es I press 'em right."

"Well," I says, "the tailor on Sixty-third satisfies us. Suppose you don't do your best this time, but just give us seventy cents' worth."

But they wasn't no chance for a bargain. He'd been in the business so long he'd become hardened and lost all regard for his fellow men.

The Missus slept, but I didn't. Instead, I

done a few problems in arithmetic. Outside o'
what she'd gave up for postcards and stamps
in Jacksonville, I'd spent two bucks for our
lunch, about two more for my shave and my
refreshments, one for a rough ride in a bus,
one more for gettin' our trunk and grips carried round, two for havin' the clo'es pressed,
and about half a buck in tips to people that
I wouldn't never see again. Somewheres near
nine dollars a day, not countin' no hotel bill,
and over two weeks of it yet to come!

Oh, you rummy game at home, at half a cent
a point!

When our clo'es come back I woke her up
and give her the figures.

"But to-day's an exception," she says.
"After this our meals will be included in the
hotel bill and we won't need to get our suits
pressed only once a week and you'll be shavin'
yourself and they won't be no bus fare when
we're stayin' in one place. Besides, we can
practise economy all spring and all summer."

"I guess we need the practise," I says.

"And if you're goin' to crab all the time about expenses," says she, "I'll wish we had of stayed home."

"That'll make it unanimous," says I.

Then she begin sobbin' about how I'd spoiled the trip and I had to promise I wouldn't think no more o' what we were spendin'. I might just as well of promised to not worry when the White Sox lost or when I'd forgot to come home to supper.

We went in the dinin'-room about six-thirty and was showed to a table where they was another couple settin'. They was husband and wife, I guess, but I don't know which was which. She was wieldin' the pencil and writin' down their order.

"I guess I'll have clams," he says.

"They disagreed with you last night," says she.

"All right," he says. "I won't try 'em. Give me cream-o'-tomato soup."

"You don't like tomatoes," she says.

"Well, I won't have no soup," says he. "A little o' the blue-fish."

"The blue-fish wasn't no good at noon," she says. "You better try the bass."

"All right, make it bass," he says. "And them sweet-breads and a little roast beef and sweet potatoes and peas and vanilla ice-cream and coffee."

"You wouldn't touch sweet-breads at home," says she, "and you can't tell what they'll be in a hotel."

"All right, cut out the sweet-breads," he says.

"I should think you'd have the stewed chicken," she says, "and leave out the roast beef."

"Stewed chicken it is," says he.

"Stewed chicken and mashed potatoes and string beans and buttered toast and coffee. Will that suit you?"

"Sure!" he says, and she give the slip to the waiter.

George looked at it long enough to of read

it three times if he could of read it once and
then went out in the kitchen and got a trayful
o' whatever was handy.

But the poor guy didn't get more'n a taste
of anything. She was watchin' him like a
hawk, and no sooner would he delve into one
victual than she'd yank the dish away from him
and tell him to remember that health was more
important than temporary happiness. I felt
so sorry for him that I couldn't enjoy my own
repast and I told the Wife that we'd have our
breakfast apart from that stricken soul if I
had to carry the case to old Al Cazar himself.

In the evenin' we strolled acrost the street
to the Ponce — that's supposed to be even
sweller yet than where we were stoppin' at.
We walked all over the place without recog-
nizin' nobody from our set. I finally warned
the Missus that if we didn't duck back to our
room I'd probably have a heart attack from
excitement; but she'd read in her Florida guide
that the decorations and pitchers was worth
goin' miles to see, so we had to stand in front

o' them for a couple hours and try to keep awake. Four or five o' them was thrillers, at that. Their names was Adventure, Discovery, Contest, and so on, but what they all should of been called was Lady Who Had Mislaid Her Clo'es.

The hotel's named after the fella that built it. He come from Spain and they say he was huntin' for some water that if he'd drunk it he'd feel young. I don't see myself how you could expect to feel young on water. But, anyway, he'd heard that this here kind o' water could be found in St. Augustine, and when he couldn't find it he went into the hotel business and got even with the United States by chargin' five dollars a day and up for a room.

Sunday mornin' we went in to breakfast early and I ast the head waiter if we could set at another table where they wasn't no convalescent and his mate. At the same time I give the said head waiter somethin' that spoke louder than words. We was showed to a place way acrost the room from where we'd been the night before. It was a table for six, but the other four didn't come into our life till that night at supper.

Meanw'ile we went sight-seein'. We visited Fort Marion, that'd be a great protection against the Germans, provided they fought with paper wads. We seen the city gate and the cathedral and the slave market, and then we took the boat over to Anastasia Island, that the ocean's on the other side of it. This trip made me homesick, because the people that was along with us on the boat looked just like the ones we'd often went with to Michigan City on the Fourth o' July. The boat landed on the bay side o' the island and from there we was drug over to the ocean side on a horse car, the the horse walkin' to one side o' the car instead of in front, so's he wouldn't get ran over.

We stuck on the beach till dinner-time and then took the chariot back to the pavilion on the bay side, where a whole family served the meal and their pigs put on a cabaret. It was the best meal I had in dear old Dixie—fresh oysters and chicken and mashed potatoes and gravy and fish and pie. And they charged two bits a plate.

"Goodness gracious!" says the Missus, when I told her the price. "This is certainly reasonable. I wonder how it happens."

"Well," I says, "the family was probably washed up here by the tide and don't know they're in Florida."

When we got back to the hotel they was only just time to clean up and go down to supper. We hadn't no sooner got seated when our table companions breezed in. It was a man about forty-five, that looked like he'd made his money in express and general haulin', and he had his wife along and both their mother-in-laws. The shirt he had on was the one he'd started from home with, if he lived in Yokohama. His womenfolks wore mournin' with a touch o' gravy here and there.

"You order for us, Jake," says one o' the ladies.

So Jake grabbed the bill o' fare and his wife took the slip and pencil and waited for the dictation.

"Let's see," he says. "How about oyster cocktail?"

"Yes," says the three Mrs. Black.

"Four oyster cocktails, then," says Jake, "and four orders o' bluepoints."

"The oysters is nice, too," says I.

They all give me a cordial smile and the ice was broke.

"Everything's good here," says Jake.

"I bet you know," I says.

He seemed pleased at the compliment and went on dictatin'.

"Four chicken soups with rice," he says, "and four o' the blue-fish and four veal chops breaded and four roast chicken and four boiled potatoes—"

But it seemed his wife would rather have sweet potatoes.

"All right," says Jake; "four boiled potatoes and four sweets. And chicken salad and some o' that tapioca puddin' and ice-cream and tea. Is that satisfactory?"

"Fine!" says one o' the mother-in-laws.

"Are you goin' to stay long?" says Mrs. Jake to my Missus.

The party addressed didn't look very clubby, but she was too polite to pull the cut direct.

"We leave to-morrow night," she says.

Nobody ast her where we was goin'.

"We leave for Palm Beach," she says.

"That's a nice place, I guess," says one o' the old ones. "More people goes there than comes here. It ain't so expensive there, I guess."

"You're some guesser," says the Missus and freezes up.

I ast Jake if he'd been to Florida before.

"No," he says; "this is our first trip, but we're makin' up for lost time. We're seein' all they is to see and havin' everything the best."

"You're havin' everything, all right," I says,

"but I don't know if it's the best or not. How long have you been here?"

"A week to-morrow," says he. "And we stay another week and then go to Ormond."

"Are you standin' the trip O. K.?" I ast him.

"Well," he says, "I don't feel quite as good as when we first come."

"Kind o' logy?" I says.

"Yes; kind o' heavy," says Jake.

"I know what you ought to do," says I. "You ought to go to a European plan hotel."

"Not w'ile this war's on," he says, "and besides, my mother's a poor sailor."

"Yes," says his mother; "I'm a very poor sailor."

"Jake's mother can't stand the water," says Mrs. Jake.

So I begun to believe that Jake's wife's mother-in-law was a total failure as a jolly tar.

Social intercourse was put an end to when the waiter staggered in with their order and our'n. The Missus seemed to of lost her appetite and just set there lookin' grouchy and tap-

pin' her fingers on the table-cloth and actin'
like she was in a hurry to get away. I didn't
eat much, neither. It was more fun watchin'.

"Well," I says, when we was out in the
lobby, "we finally got acquainted with some
real people."

"Real people!" says the Missus, curlin' her
lip. "What did you talk to 'em for?"

"I couldn't resist," I says. "Anybody that'd
order four oyster cocktails and four rounds o'
blue-points is worth knowin'."

"Well," she says, "if they're there when we
go in to-morrow mornin' we'll get our table
changed again or you can eat with 'em alone."

But they was absent from the breakfast
board.

"They're probably stayin' in bed to-day to
get their clo'es washed," says the Missus.

"Or maybe they're sick," I says. "A change
of oysters affects some people."

I was for goin' over to the island again and
gettin' another o' them quarter banquets, but

the program was for us to walk round town all mornin' and take a ride in the afternoon.

First, we went to St. George Street and visited the oldest house in the United States. Then we went to Hospital Street and seen the oldest house in the United States. Then we turned the corner and went down St. Francis Street and inspected the oldest house in the United States. Then we dropped into a soda fountain and I had an egg phosphate, made from the oldest egg in the Western Hemisphere. We passed up lunch and got into a carriage drawn by the oldest horse in Florida, and we rode through the country all afternoon and the driver told us some o' the oldest jokes in the book. He felt it was only fair to give his customers a good time when he was chargin' a dollar an hour, and he had his gags rehearsed so's he could tell the same one a thousand times and never change a word. And the horse knowed where the point come in every one and stopped to laugh.

We done our packin' before supper, and by the time we got to our table Jake and the mourners was through and gone. We didn't have to ask the waiter if they'd been there. He was perspirin' like an evangelist.

After supper we said good-by to the night clerk and twenty-two bucks. Then we bought ourself another ride in the motor-bus and landed at the station ten minutes before train-time; so we only had an hour to wait for the train.

Say, I don't know how many stations they is between New York and San Francisco, but they's twice as many between St. Augustine and Palm Beach. And our train stopped twice and started twice at every one. I give up tryin' to sleep and looked out the window, amusin' myself by readin' the names o' the different stops. The only one that expressed my sentiments was Eau Gallie. We was an hour and a half late pullin' out o' that joint and I figured we'd be two hours to the bad gettin' into our destination. But the guy that made out the

time-table must of had the engineer down pat,
because when we went acrost the bridge over
Lake Worth and landed at the Poinciana de-
pot, we was ten minutes ahead o' time.

They was about two dozen uniformed Ephs
on the job to meet us. And when I seen 'em
all grab for our baggage with one hand and
hold the other out, face up, I knowed why they
called it Palm Beach.

IV

The Poinciana station's a couple hundred
yards from one end o' the hotel, and that means
it's close to five miles from the clerk's desk. By
the time we'd registered and been gave our key
and marathoned another five miles or so to
where our room was located at, I was about
ready for the inquest. But the Missus was full
o' pep and wild to get down to breakfast and
look over our stable mates. She says we would
eat without changin' our clo'es; people'd forgive us for not dressin' up on account o' just

119

gettin' there. W'ile she was lookin' out the window at the royal palms and buzzards, I moseyed round the room inspectin' where the different doors led to. Pretty near the first one I opened went into a private bath.

"Here," I says; "they've give us the wrong room."

Then my wife seen it and begin to squeal.

"Goody!" she says. "We've got a bath! We've got a bath!"

"But," says I, "they promised we wouldn't have none. It must be a mistake."

"Never you mind about a mistake," she says. "This is our room and they can't chase us out of it."

"We'll chase ourself out," says I. "Rooms with a bath is fifteen and sixteen dollars and up. Rooms without no bath is bad enough."

"We'll keep this room or I won't stay here," she says.

"All right, you win," I says; but I didn't mean it.

I made her set in the lobby down-stairs w'ile

I went to the clerk pretendin' that I had to see about our trunk.

"Say," I says to him, "you've made a bad mistake. You told your man in Chicago that we couldn't have no room with a bath, and now you've give us one."

"You're lucky," he says. "A party who had a bath ordered for these two weeks canceled their reservation and now you've got it."

"Lucky, am I?" I says. "And how much is the luck goin' to cost me?"

"It'll be seventeen dollars per day for that room," he says, and turned away to hide a blush.

I went back to the Wife.

"Do you know what we're payin' for that room?" I says. "We're payin' seventeen dollars."

"Well," she says, "our meals is throwed in."

"Yes," says I, "and the hotel furnishes a key."

"You promised in St. Augustine," she says,

"that you wouldn't worry no more about expenses."

Well, rather than make a scene in front o' the bellhops and the few millionaires that was able to be about at that hour o' the mornin', I just says "All right!" and led her into the dinin'-room.

The head waiter met us at the door and turned us over to his assistant. Then some more assistants took hold of us one at a time and we was relayed to a beautiful spot next door to the kitchen and bounded on all sides by posts and pillars. It was all right for me, but a whole lot too private for the Missus; so I had to call the fella that had been our pacemaker on the last lap.

"We don't like this table," I says.

"It's the only one I can give you," he says.

I slipped him half a buck.

"Come to think of it," he says, "I believe they's one I forgot all about."

And he moved us way up near the middle o' the place.

Say, you ought to seen that dinin'-room! From one end of it to the other is a toll call, and if a man that was settin' at the table farthest from the kitchen ordered roast lamb he'd get mutton. At that, they was crowded for fair and it kept the head waiters hustlin' to find trough space for one and all.

It was round nine o'clock when we put in our modest order for orange juice, oatmeal, liver and bacon, and cakes and coffee, and a quarter to ten or so when our waiter returned from the nearest orange grove with Exhibit A. We amused ourself meanw'ile by givin' our neighbors the once over and wonderin' which o' them was goin' to pal with us. As far as I could tell from the glances we received, they wasn't no immediate danger of us bein' annoyed by attentions.

They was only a few womenfolks on deck and they was dressed pretty quiet; so quiet that the Missus was scared she'd shock 'em with the sport skirt she'd bought in Chi. Later on in the day, when the girls come out for their dress parade, the Missus' costume made about as much noise as eatin' marshmallows in a foundry.

After breakfast we went to the room for a change o' raiment. I put on my white trousers and wished to heaven that the sun'd go under a cloud till I got used to tellin' people without words just where my linen began and I left off. The rest o' my outfit was white shoes that hurt, and white sox, and a two-dollar silk shirt that showed up a zebra, and a red tie and a soft collar and a blue coat. The Missus wore a sport suit that I won't try and describe—you'll probably see it on her sometime in the next five years.

We went down-stairs again and out on the porch, where some o' the old birds was takin' a sun bath.

"Where now?" I says.

"The beach, o' course," says the Missus.

"Where is it at?" I ast her.

"I suppose," she says, "that we'll find it somewheres near the ocean."

"I don't believe you can stand this climate," says I.

"The ocean," she says, "must be down at the end o' that avenue, where most everybody seems to be headed."

"Havin' went to our room and back twice, I don't feel like another five-mile hike," I says.

"It ain't no five miles," she says; "but let's ride, anyway."

"Come on," says I, pointin' to a street-car that was standin' in the middle o' the avenue.

"Oh, no," she says. "I've watched and found out that the real people takes them funny-lookin' wheel chairs."

I was wonderin' what she meant when one o' them pretty near run over us. It was part bicycle, part go-cart and part African. In the one we dodged they was room for one passenger, but some o' them carried two.

"I wonder what they'd soak us for the trip," I says.

"Not more'n a dime, I don't believe," says the Missus.

But when we'd hired one and been w'isked down under the palms and past the golf field to the bath-house, we was obliged to part with fifty cents legal and tender.

"I feel much refreshed," I says. "I believe when it comes time to go back I'll be able to walk."

The bath-house is acrost the street from the other hotel, the Breakers, that the man had told us was full for the season. Both buildin's fronts on the ocean; and, boy, it's some ocean! I bet they's fish in there that never seen each other!

"Oh, let's go bathin' right away!" says the Missus.

"Our suits is up to the other beanery," says I, and I was glad of it. They wasn't nothin' temptin' to me about them man-eatin' waves.

But the Wife's a persistent cuss.

"We won't go to-day," she says, "but we'll go in the bath-house and get some rooms for to-morrow.

The bath-house porch was a ringer for the

Follies. Here and down on the beach was where you seen the costumes at this time o' day. I was so busy rubberin' that I passed the entrance door three times without noticin' it. From the top o' their heads to the bottom o' their feet the girls was a mess o' colors. They wasn't no two dressed alike and if any one o' them had of walked down State Street we'd of had an epidemic o' stiff neck to contend with in Chi. Finally the Missus grabbed me and hauled me into the office.

"Two private rooms," she says to the clerk. "One lady and one gent."

"Five dollars a week apiece," he says. "But we're all filled up."

"You ought to be all locked up!" I says.

"Will you have anything open to-morrow?" ast the Missus.

"I think I can fix you then," he says.

"What do we get for the five?" I ast him.

"Private room and we take care o' your bathin' suit," says he.

"How much if you don't take care o' the

suit?" I ast him. "My suit's been gettin' along fine with very little care."

"Five dollars a week apiece," he says, "and if you want the rooms you better take 'em, because they're in big demand."

By the time we'd closed this grand bargain, everybody'd moved offen the porch and down to the water, where a couple dozen o' them went in for a swim and the rest set and watched. They was a long row o' chairs on the beach for spectators and we was just goin' to flop into two o' them when another bandit come up and told us it'd cost a dime apiece per hour.

"We're goin' to be here two weeks," I says. "Will you sell us two chairs?"

He wasn't in no comical mood, so we sunk down on the sand and seen the show from there. We had plenty o' company that preferred these kind o' seats free to the chairs at ten cents a whack.

Besides the people that was in the water gettin' knocked down by the waves and pretendin' like they enjoyed it, about half o' the gang on the sand was wearin' bathin' suits just to be clubby. You could tell by lookin' at the suits that they hadn't never been wet and wasn't intended for no such ridic'lous purpose. I wisht I could describe 'em to you, but it'd take a female to do it right.

One little girl, either fourteen or twenty-four, had white silk slippers and sox that come pretty near up to her ankles, and from there to her knees it was just plain Nature. North-bound from her knees was a pair o' bicycle trousers that disappeared when they come to the bottom of her Mother Hubbard. This here garment was a thing without no neck or sleeves that begin bulgin' at the top and spread out gradual all the way down, like a croquette. To top her off, she had a jockey cap; and—believe me—I'd of played her mount acrost the board. They was plenty o' class in the field with her, but nothin' that approached her speed. Later on I seen her several times round the hotel, wearin' somethin' near the same outfit, without the jockey cap and with longer croquettes.

We set there in the sand till people begun to get up and leave. Then we trailed along back o' them to the Breakers' porch, where they was music to dance and stuff to inhale.

"We'll grab a table," I says to the Missus. "I'm dyin' o' thirst."

But I was allowed to keep on dyin'.

"I can serve you somethin' soft," says the waiter.

"I'll bet you can't!" I says.

"You ain't got no locker here?" he says.

"What do you mean—locker?" I ast him.

"It's the locker liquor law," he says. "We can serve you a drink if you own your own bottles."

"I'd just as soon own a bottle," I says. "I'll become the proprietor of a bottle o' beer."

"It'll take three or four hours to get it for you," he says, "and you'd have to order it through the order desk. If you're stoppin' at one o' the hotels and want a drink once in a w'ile, you better get busy and put in an order."

So I had to watch the Missus put away a glass of orange juice that cost forty cents and was just the same size as they give us for breakfast free for nothin'. And, not havin' had nothin' to make me forget that my feet hurt, I was obliged to pay another four bits for an Afromobile to cart us back to our own boardin' house.

"Well," says the Missus when we got there, "it's time to wash up and go to lunch."

"Wash up and go to lunch, then," I says; "but I'm goin' to investigate this here locker liquor or liquor locker law."

So she got her key and beat it, and I limped to the bar.

"I want a highball," I says to the boy.

"What's your number?" says he.

"It varies," I says. "Sometimes I can hold twenty and sometimes four or five makes me sing."

"I mean, have you got a locker here?" he says.

"No; but I want to get one," says I.

"The gent over there to the desk will fix you," says he.

So over to the desk I went and ast for a locker.

"What do you drink?" ast the gent.

"I'm from Chicago," I says. "I drink bourbon."

"What's your name and room number?" he says, and I told him.

Then he ast me how often did I shave and what did I think o' the Kaiser and what my name was before I got married, and if I had any intentions of ever running an elevator. Finally he says I was all right.

"I'll order you some bourbon," he says. "Anything else?"

I was goin' to say no, but I happened to remember that the Wife generally always wants a bronix before dinner. So I had to also put in a bid for a bottle o' gin and bottles o' the Vermouth brothers, Tony and Pierre. It wasn't till later that I appreciated what a grand law this here law was. When I got my drinks I paid ten cents apiece for 'em for service, besides payin' for the bottles o' stuff to drink. And, besides that, about every third highball or bronix I ordered, the waiter'd bring back word that I was just out of ingredients and then they'd be another delay w'ile they sent to the garage for more. If they had that law all over the country they'd soon be an end o' drinkin', because everybody'd get so mad they'd kill each other.

My cross-examination had took quite a long time, but when I got to my room the Wife wasn't back from lunch yet and I had to cover the Marathon route all over again and look her up. We only had the one key to the room, and o' course couldn't expect no more'n that at the price.

The Missus had bought one o' the daily programs they get out and she knowed just what we had to do the rest o' the day.

"For the next couple hours," she says, "we can suit ourself."

"All right," says I. "It suits me to take off my shoes and lay down."

"I'll rest, too," she says; "but at half past four we have to be in the Cocoanut Grove for tea and dancin'. And then we come back to the room and dress for dinner. Then we eat and then we set around till the evenin' dance starts. Then we dance till we're ready for bed."

"Who do we dance all these dances with?" I ast her.

"With whoever we get acquainted with," she says.

"All right," says I; "but let's be careful."

Well, we took our nap and then we followed schedule and had our tea in the Cocoanut Grove. You know how I love tea! My feet was still achin' and the Missus couldn't talk me into no dance.

When we'd set there an hour and was saturated with tea, the Wife says it was time to go up and change into our Tuxedos. I was all in when we reached the room and willin' to even pass up supper and nestle in the hay, but I was informed that the biggest part o' the day's doin's was yet to come. So from six o'clock till after seven I wrestled with studs, and hooks and eyes that didn't act like they'd ever met before and wasn't anxious to get acquainted, and then down we went again to the dinin'-room.

"How about a little bronix before the feed?" I says.

"It would taste good," says the Missus.

So I called Eph and give him the order. In somethin' less than half an hour he come back empty-handed.

"You ain't got no cocktail stuff," he says.

"I certainly have," says I. "I ordered it early this afternoon."

"Where at?" he ast me.

"Over in the bar," I says.

"Oh, the regular bar!" he says. "That don't count. You got to have stuff at the service bar to get it served in here."

"I ain't as thirsty as I thought I was," says I.

"Me, neither," says the Missus.

So we went ahead and ordered our meal, and w'ile we was waitin' for it a young couple come and took the other two chairs at our table. They didn't have to announce through a megaphone that they was honeymooners. It was wrote all over 'em. They was reachin' under the table for each other's hand every other minute, and when they wasn't doin' that they was smilin' at each other or gigglin' at nothin'. You couldn't feel that good and be payin' seventeen dollars a day for room and board unless you was just married or somethin'.

I thought at first their company'd be fun, but after a few meals it got like the southern cookin' and begun to undermine the health.

The conversation between they and us was what you could call limited. It took place the next day at lunch. The young husband thought he was about to take a bite o' the entry, which happened to be roast mutton with sirup; but he couldn't help from lookin' at her at the same time and his empty fork started for his face prongs up.

"Look out for your eye," I says.

He dropped the fork and they both blushed till you could see it right through the sunburn. Then they give me a Mexican look and our acquaintance was at an end.

This first night, when we was through eatin', we wandered out in the lobby and took seats where we could watch the passin' show. The men was all dressed like me, except I was up to date and had on a mushroom shirt, w'ile they was sportin' the old-fashioned concrete bosom. The women's dresses begun at the top with a belt, and some o' them stopped at the mezzanine floor, w'ile others went clear down to the basement and helped keep the rugs clean. They was one that must of thought it was the Fourth o' July. From the top of her head to where the top of her bathin' suit had left off, she was a red, red rose. From there to the top of her gown was white, and her gown, what they was of it—was blue.

"My!" says the Missus. "What stunnin' gowns!"

"Yes," I says; "and you could have one just like 'em if you'd take the shade offen the piano lamp at home and cut it down to the right size."

Round ten o'clock we wandered in the Palm Garden, where the dancin' had been renewed. The Wife wanted to plunge right in the mazes o' the foxy trot.

"I'll take some courage first," says I. And then was when I found out that it cost you ten cents extra besides the tip to pay for a drink that you already owned in fee simple.

Well, I guess we must of danced about six dances together and had that many quarrels before she was ready to go to bed. And oh, how grand that old hay-pile felt when I finally bounced into it!

The next day we went to the ocean at the legal hour—half past eleven. I never had so much fun in my life. The surf was runnin' high, I heard 'em say; and I don't know which I'd rather do, go bathin' in the ocean at Palm Beach when the surf is runnin' high, or have a dentist get one o' my molars ready for a big inlay at a big outlay. Once in a w'ile I managed to not get throwed on my head when a wave hit me. As for swimmin', you had just as much chance as if you was at State and Madison at the noon hour. And before I'd been in a minute they was enough salt in my different features to keep the Blackstone hotel runnin' all through the onion season.

The Missus enjoyed it just as much as me. She tried to pretend at first, and when she got floored she'd give a squeal that was supposed to mean heavenly bliss. But after she'd been bruised from head to feet and her hair looked and felt like spinach with French dressin', and she'd drank all she could hold o' the Gulf Stream, she didn't resist none when I drug her in to shore and staggered with her up to our private rooms at five a week per each.

Without consultin' her, I went to the desk at the Casino and told 'em they could have them rooms back.

"All right," says the clerk, and turned our keys over to the next in line.

"How about a refund?" I ast him; but he was waitin' on somebody else.

After that we done our bathin' in the tub. But we was down to the beach every morning at eleven-thirty to watch the rest o' them get batted round.

And at half past twelve every day we'd follow the crowd to the Breakers' porch and dance together, the Missus and I. Then it'd be back to the other hostelry, sometimes limpin' and sometimes in an Afromobile, and a drink or two in the Palm Garden before lunch. And after lunch we'd lay down; or we'd pay some Eph two or three dollars to pedal us through the windin' jungle trail, that was every bit as wild as the Art Institute; or we'd ferry acrost Lake Worth to West Palm Beach and take in a movie, or we'd stand in front o' the portable Fifth Avenue stores w'ile the Missus wished she could have this dress or that hat, or somethin' else that she wouldn't of looked at if she'd been home and in her right mind. But always at half past four we had to live up to the rules and be in the Cocoanut Grove for tea and some more foxy trottin'. And then it was dress for dinner, eat dinner, watch the parade and wind up the glorious day with more dancin'.

I bet you any amount you name that the Castles in their whole life haven't danced together as much as I and the Missus did at Palm Beach. I'd of gave five dollars if even one o' the waiters had took her offen my hands for one dance. But I knowed that if I made the offer public they'd of been a really serious quarrel between us instead o' just the minor brawls occasioned by steppin' on each other's feet.

She made a discovery one night. She found out that they was a place called the Beach Club where most o' the real people disappeared to every evenin' after dinner. She says we would have to go there too.

"But I ain't a member," I says.

"Then find out how you get to be one," she says.

So to the Beach Club I went and made inquiries.

"You'll have to be introduced by a guy that already belongs," says the man at the door.

"Who belongs?" I ast him.

"Hundreds o' people," he says. "Who do you know?"

"Two waiters, two barkeepers and one elevator boy," I says.

He laughed, but his laugh didn't get me no membership card and I had to dance three or four extra times the next day to square myself with the Missus.

She made another discovery and it cost me six bucks. She found out that, though the meals in the regular dinin'-room was included in the triflin' rates per day, the real people had at least two o' their meals in the garden grill and paid extra for 'em. We tried it for one meal and I must say I enjoyed it—all but the check.

"We can't keep up that clip," I says to her.

"We could," says she, "if you wasn't spendin' so much on your locker."

"The locker's a matter o' life and death," I

says. "They ain't no man in the world that could dance as much with their own wife as I do and live without liquid stimulus."

When we'd been there four days she got to be on speakin' terms with the ladies' maid that hung round the lobby and helped put the costumes back on when they slipped off. From this here maid the Missus learned who was who, and the information was relayed to me as soon as they was a chance. We'd be settin' on the porch when I'd feel an elbow in my ribs all of a sudden. I'd look up at who was passin' and then try and pretend I was excited.

"Who is it?" I'd whisper.

"That's Mrs. Vandeventer," the Wife'd say. "Her husband's the biggest street-car conductor in Philadelphia."

Or somebody'd set beside us at the beach or in the Palm Garden and my ribs would be all battered up before the Missus was calm enough to tip me off.

"The Vincents," she'd say; "the canned prune people."

It was a little bit thrillin' at first to be rubbin' elbows with all them celeb's; but it got so finally that I could walk out o' the dinin'-room right behind Scotti, the opera singer, without forgettin' that my feet hurt.

The Washington's Birthday Ball brought 'em all together at once, and the Missus pointed out eight and nine at a time and got me so mixed up that I didn't know Pat Vanderbilt from Maggie Rockefeller. The only one you couldn't make no mistake about was a Russian count that you couldn't pronounce. He was buyin' bay mules or somethin' for the Russian government, and he was in ambush.

"They say he can't hardly speak a word of English," says the Missus.

"If I knowed the word for barber shop in Russia," says I, "I'd tell him they was one in this hotel."

V

In our mail box the next mornin' they was a notice that our first week was up and all we owed was one hundred and forty-six dollars and fifty cents. The bill for room and meals was one hundred and nineteen dollars. The rest was for gettin' clo'es pressed and keepin' the locker damp.

I didn't have no appetite for breakfast. I told the Wife I'd wait up in the room and for her to come when she got through. When she blew in I had my speech prepared.

"Look here," I says; "this is our eighth day in Palm Beach society. You're on speakin' terms with a maid and I've got acquainted with half a dozen o' the male hired help. It's cost us about a hundred and sixty-five dollars, includin' them private rooms down to the Casino and our Afromobile trips, and this and that. You know a whole lot o' swell people by sight, but you can't talk to 'em. It'd be just as much satisfaction and hundreds o' dollars cheaper to look up their names in the telephone directory at home; then phone to 'em and, when you got 'em, tell 'em it was the wrong number. That way, you'd get 'em to speak to you at least.

"As for sport," I says, "we don't play golf and we don't play tennis and we don't swim. We go through the same program o' doin' nothin' every day. We dance, but we don't never change partners. For twelve dollars I could buy a phonograph up home and I and you could trot round the livin'-room all evenin' without no danger o' havin' some o' them fancy birds cave our shins in. And we could have twice as much liquid refreshments up there at about a twentieth the cost.

"That Gould I met on the train comin' down," I says, "was a even bigger liar than I give him credit for. He says that when he was here people pestered him to death by comin' up and speakin' to him. We ain't had to dodge nobody or hide behind a cocoanut tree to remain exclusive. He says Palm Beach was too common for him. What he should of said was that it was too lonesome. If they was just one white man here that'd listen to my stuff I wouldn't have no kick. But it ain't no pleasure tellin' stories to the Ephs. They laugh whether it's good or not, and then want a dime for laughin'.

"As for our clo'es," I says, "they would be all right for a couple o' days' stay. But the dames round here, and the men, too, has somethin' different to put on for every mornin', afternoon and night. You've wore your two evenin' gowns so much that I just have to snap my finger at the hooks and they go and grab the right eyes.

"The meals would be grand," I says, "if the cook didn't keep gettin' mixed up and puttin' puddin' sauce on the meat and gravy on the pie.

"I'm glad we've been to Palm Beach," I says. "I wouldn't of missed it for nothin'. But the ocean won't be no different to-morrow than it was yesterday, and the same for the daily program. It don't even rain here, to give us a little variety.

"Now what do you say," I says, "to us just

settlin' this bill, and whatever we owe since then, and beatin' it out o' here just as fast as we can go?"

The Missus didn't say nothin' for a w'ile. She was too busy cryin'. She knowed that what I'd said was the truth, but she wouldn't give up without a struggle.

"Just three more days," she says finally. "If we don't meet somebody worth meetin' in the next three days I'll go wherever you want to take me."

"All right," I says; "three more days it is. What's a little matter o' sixty dollars?"

Well, in them next two days and a half she done some desperate flirtin', but as it was all with women I didn't get jealous. She picked out some o' the E-light o' Chicago and tried every trick she could think up. She told 'em their noses was shiny and offered 'em her powder. She stepped on their white shoes just so's to get a chance to beg their pardon. She told 'em their clo'es was unhooked, and then unhooked 'em so's she could hook 'em up again.

She tried to loan 'em her finger-nail tools. When she seen one fannin' herself she'd say: "Excuse me, Mrs. So-and-So; but we got the coolest room in the hotel, and I'd be glad to have you go up there and quit perspirin'." But not a rise did she get.

Not till the afternoon o' the third day o' grace. And I don't know if I ought to tell you this or not—only I'm sure you won't spill it nowheres.

We'd went up in our room after lunch. I was tired out and she was discouraged. We'd set round for over an hour, not sayin' or doin' nothin'.

I wanted to talk about the chance of us gettin' away the next mornin', but I didn't dast bring up the subject.

The Missus complained of it bein' hot and opened the door to leave the breeze go through. She was settin' in a chair near the doorway, pretendin' to read the *Palm Beach News*. All of a sudden she jumped up and kind o' hissed at me.

"What's the matter?" I says, springin' from the lounge.

"Come here!" she says, and went out the door into the hall.

I got there as fast as I could, thinkin' it was a rat or a fire. But the Missus just pointed to a lady walkin' away from us, six or seven doors down.

"It's Mrs. Potter," she says; "*the* Mrs. Potter from Chicago!"

"Oh!" I says, puttin' all the excitement I could into my voice.

And I was just startin' back into the room when I seen Mrs. Potter stop and turn round and come to'rd us. She stopped again maybe twenty feet from where the Missus was standin'.

"Are you on this floor?" she says.

The Missus shook like a leaf.

"Yes," says she, so low you couldn't hardly hear her.

"Please see that they's some towels put in 559," says *the* Mrs. Potter from Chicago.

VI

About five o'clock the Wife quieted down and I thought it was safe to talk to her. "I've been readin' in the guide about a pretty river trip," I says. "We can start from here on the boat to-morrow mornin'. They run to Fort Pierce to-morrow and stay there to-morrow night. The next day they go from Fort Pierce to Rockledge, and the day after that from Rockledge to Daytona. The fare's only five dollars apiece. And we can catch a north-bound train at Daytona."

"All right, I don't care," says the Missus.

So I left her and went down-stairs and acrost the street to ask Mr. Foster. Ask Mr. Foster happened to be a girl. She sold me the boat tickets and promised she would reserve a room with bath for us at Fort Pierce, where we was to spend the followin' night. I bet she knowed all the w'ile that rooms with a bath in Fort Pierce is scarcer than toes on a sturgeon.

I went back to the room and helped with the

packin' in an advisory capacity. Neither one of us had the heart to dress for dinner. We ordered somethin' sent up and got soaked an extra dollar for service. But we was past carin' for a little thing like that.

At nine o'clock next mornin' the good ship *Constitution* stopped at the Poinciana dock w'ile we piled aboard. One bellhop was down to see us off and it cost me a quarter to get that much attention. Mrs. Potter must of overslept herself.

The boat was loaded to the guards and I ain't braggin' when I say that we was the best-lookin' people aboard. And as for manners, why, say, old Bill Sykes could of passed off for Henry Chesterfield in that gang! Each one o' them occupied three o' the deck chairs and sprayed orange juice all over their neighbors. We could of talked to plenty o' people here, all right; they were as clubby a gang as I ever seen. But I was afraid if I said somethin' they'd have to answer; and, with their mouths as full o' citrus fruit as they was, the results might of been fatal to my light suit.

We went up the lake to a canal and then through it to Indian River. The boat run aground every few minutes and had to be pried loose. About twelve o'clock a cullud gemman come up on deck and told us lunch was ready. At half past one he served it at a long family table in the cabin. As far as I was concerned, he might as well of left it on the stove. Even if you could of bit into the food, a glimpse of your fellow diners would of strangled your appetite.

After the repast I called the Missus aside.

"Somethin' tells me we're not goin' to live through three days o' this," I says. "What about takin' the train from Fort Pierce and beatin' it for Jacksonville, and then home?"

"But that'd get us to Chicago too quick," says she. "We told people how long we was goin' to be gone and if we got back ahead o' time they'd think they was somethin' queer."

"They's too much queer on this boat," I says. "But you're goin' to have your own way from now on."

We landed in Fort Pierce about six. It was only two or three blocks to the hotel, but when they laid out that part o' town they overlooked some o' the modern conveniences, includin' sidewalks. We staggered through the sand with our grips and sure had worked up a hunger by the time we reached Ye Inn.

"Got reservations for us here?" I ast the clerk.

"Yes," he says, and led us to 'em in person.

The room he showed us didn't have no bath, or even a chair that you could set on w'ile you pulled off your socks.

"Where's the bath?" I ast him.

"This way," he says, and I followed him down the hall, outdoors and up an alley.

Finally we come to a bathroom complete in all details, except that it didn't have no door. I went back to the room, got the Missus and went down to supper. Well, sir, I wish you could of been present at that supper. The choice o' meats was calves' liver and onions or calves' liver and onions. And I bet if them calves had of been still livin' yet they could of gave us some personal reminiscences about Garfield.

The Missus give the banquet one look and then laughed for the first time in several days.

"The guy that named this burg got the capitals mixed," I says. "It should of been Port Fierce."

And she laughed still heartier. Takin' advantage, I says:

"How about the train from here to Jacksonville?"

"You win!" says she. "We can't get home too soon to suit me."

VII

The mornin' we landed in Chicago it was about eight above and a wind was comin' offen the Lake a mile a minute. But it didn't feaze us.

"Lord!" says the Missus. "Ain't it grand to be home!"

"You said somethin'," says I. "But wouldn't it of been grander if we hadn't never left?"

"I don't know about that," she says. "I think we both of us learned a lesson."

"Yes," I says; "and the tuition wasn't only a matter o' close to seven hundred bucks!"

"Oh," says she, "we'll get that back easy!"

"How?" I ast her. "Do you expect some tips on the market from Mrs. Potter and the rest o' your new friends?"

"No," she says. "We'll win it. We'll win it in the rummy game with the Hatches."

THE WATER CURE

WHEN it comes to makin' matches I hand it to the women. When it comes to breakin' 'em leave it to the handsomer sex.

The thirteenth o' June didn't light on a Friday, but old Tuesday come through in the pinch with just as good results. Dear little Sister-in-law Bess blew in on the afternoon train from Wabash. She says she was makin' us a surprise visit. The surprise affected me a good deal like the one that was pulled on Napoleon at Waterloo, Ia.

"How long are you goin' to light up our home?" I ast her at the supper table.

"I haven't made up my mind," says she.

"That's all you've missed, then," I says.

"Don't mind him!" says my Missus. "He's just a tease. You look grand and we're both tickled to death to have you here. You may stay with us all summer."

"No question about that," I says. "Not only may, but li'ble to."

"If I do," says Bess, "it'll be on my sister's account, not yourn."

"But I'm the baby that settles your sister's account," I says; "and it was some account after you left us last winter. With your visit and our cute little trip to Palm Beach, I'm not what you'd call cramped for pocket space."

"I guess I can pay my board," says Bess.

"I guess you won't!" says the Wife.

"The second guess is always better," says I.

"As for you entertainin' me, I don't expect nothin' like that," says Bess.

"If you was lookin' for a quiet time," I says, "you made a big mistake by leavin' Wabash."

"And I'm not lookin' for no quiet time, neither," Bess says right back at me.

"Well," says I, "about the cheapest noisy time I can recommend is to go over and set under the elevated."

"Maybe Bess has somethin' up in her sleeve,"

the Missus says, smilin'. "You ain't the only man in Chicago."

"I'm the only one she knows," says I, "outside o' that millionaire scenario writer that had us all in misery last winter. And I wouldn't say he was over-ardent after he'd knew her a week."

Then the Wife winked at me to close up and I didn't get the dope till we was alone together.

"They correspond," she told me.

"Absolutely," says I.

"I mean they been writin' letters to each other," says the Missus.

"Who's been buyin' Bishop's stamps?" I ast her.

"I guess a man can buy his own stamps when he gets ten thousand a year," says she. "Anyway, the reason Bess is here is to see him."

"Is it illegal for him to go to Wabash and see her?" I says.

"He's too busy to go to Wabash," the Wife says.

"I don't see how a man could be too busy for that," says I.

"She phoned him this noon," says the Missus. "He couldn't come over here to-night, but to-morrow he's goin' to take her to the ball game."

"Where all the rest o' the busy guys hangs out," I says. "Aren't the White Sox havin' enough bad luck without him?"

That reminded me that I'd came home before the final extras was out; so I put on my hat and went over to Tim's to look at the score-board. It took me till one A. M. to memorize the batteries and everything. The Wife was still awake yet when I got home and I had enough courage to resume hostilities.

"If what you told me about Bishop and Bess is true," I says, "I guess I'll pack up and go fishin' for the rest o' the summer."

"And leave me to starve, I suppose!" says she.

"Bishop'll take care of the both o' you," I says. "If he don't I'll send you home a couple o' carp."

"If you go and leave me it's the last time!" she says. "And it shows you don't care nothin' about me."

"I care about you, all right," I says; "but not enough to be drove crazy in my own house."

"They's nothin' for you to go crazy about," she says. "If Bess and Mr. Bishop wants to tie up leave 'em alone and forget about 'em."

"I'd like nothin' better," I says; "but you know they'll give us no chance to forget about 'em."

"Why not?" she ast me.

"Because they'd starve to death without us," I says.

"Starve to death!" she says. "On ten thousand a year!"

"Now here!" I says. "Who told you he got that trifle?"

"He did," says the Wife.

"And how do you know he wasn't overestimatin'?" I ast her.

"You mean how do I know he wasn't lyin'?" she says.

"Yes," says I.

"Because he's a gentleman," she says.

"And he told you that, too?" I ast.

"No," she says. "I could tell that by lookin' at him."

"All right, Clara Voyant!" I says. "And maybe you can tell by lookin' at me how much money he borrowed off'n me and never give back."

"When? How much?" she says.

"One at a time, please," says I. "The amount o' the cash transaction was a twenty-dollar gold certificate. And the time he shook me down was the evenin' he took us to hear *Ada,* and was supposed to be payin' for it."

"I can't believe it," says the Missus.

"All right," I says. "When he brings Bessie home from the ball game to-morrow I'll put it up to him right in front o' you."

"No! You mustn't do that!" she says. "I won't have him insulted."

"You would have him insulted if I knowed how to go about it," I says.

"You stayed over to Tim's too long," says the Wife.

"Yes," says I, "and I made arrangements to stay over there every time Bishop comes here."

"Suit yourself," she says, and pretended like she was asleep.

Well, the next mornin' I got to thinkin' over what I'd said and wonderin' if I'd went too strong. But I couldn't see where. This bird was a dude that had got acquainted with Bessie on the train when she was on her way here to visit us last winter. He'd infested the house all the while she was with us. He'd gave us that ten-thousand-dollar yarn and told us he made it by writin' movin'-pitcher plays, but we never seen none o' them advertised and never run into anybody that had heard of him.

The Missus had picked him out for Bess the minute she seen him. Bessie herself had fell for him strong. To keep 'em both from droppin' cyanide in my gruel, I'd took him along with us to see *The Love o' Three Kings,* besides buyin' his groceries and provisions for pretty near a week and standin' for the upkeep on the davenport where him and Bess held hands. Finally, after he'd went six days without submittin' even circumstantial evidence that he'd ever had a dime, I bullied him into sayin' he'd give us a party.

Then they'd been an argument over where he'd take us. He'd suggested a vaudeville show, but I jumped on that with both feet. Bessie held out for a play, but I told her they wasn't none that I'd leave a young unmarried sister-in-law o' mine go to.

"Oh," Bess had said, "they must be some that's perfectly genteel."

"Yes," I told her, "there is some; but they're not worth seein'."

So they'd ast what was left and I'd mentioned grand opera.

"They're worse than plays, the most o' them," was the Wife's cut-in.

"But all the risky parts is sang in Latin and Greek," I'd said.

Well, Bishop put up a great fight, but I

wouldn't break ground, and finally he says he would take us to opera if he could get tickets.

"I'm down-town every day," I'd told him. "I'll have 'em reserved for you."

But no; he wouldn't see me put to all that trouble for the world; he'd do the buyin' himself.

So *Ada* was what he took us to on a Sunday night, when the seats was cut to half price. And when I and him went out between acts to try the limes he catched me with my guard down and frisked the twenty.

Now Bess had tipped off the Wife that her and Bishop was practically engaged, but the night after *Ada* was the last night of her visit and Bishop hadn't never came round. So Bessie'd cried all night and tried to get him by phone before she left next day; but neither o' them two acts done her any good. It looked like he was all through. On the way to the train Bess and the Missus had ruined three or four handkerchiefs and called the bird every low-down flirt they could think of. I didn't say a word; nor did I perfume my linen with brine.

Here, though, was Bess back in town and Old Man Short makin' up to her again. And they'd been correspondin'. The second time was li'ble to take, unless outside brains come to the rescue.

If I'd thought for a minute that they'd leave us out of it and go away somewhere by themself and live—the North Side, or one o' the suburbs, or Wabash—I wouldn't of cared how many times they married each other. But I had him spotted for a loafer that couldn't earn a livin', and I knowed what the maritile nuptials between Bess and he meant—it meant that I and the Missus would have all the pleasures o' conductin' a family hotel without the pain o' makin' out receipts.

Now I always wanted a boy and a girl, but I wanted 'em to be kind o' youngish when I got 'em. I never craved addin' a married couple to my family—not even if they was crazy about rummy and paid all their bills. And when it come to Bishop and Bess, well, they was just as welcome to my home as Villa and all the little Villains.

It wasn't just Bishop, with his quaint habit o' never havin' car fare. Bess, in her way, was as much of a liability. You couldn't look at her without a slight relapse. She had two complexions—A. M. and P. M. The P. M. wasn't so bad, but she could of put the other in her vanity box for a mirror. Her nose curved a little away from the batsman and wasn't no wider than a Julienne potato, and yet it had to draw in to get between her eyes. Her teeth was real pretty and she always kept her lips ajar. But the baseball reporters named Matty's favorite delivery after her chin, and from there down the curves was taboo.

Where she made a hit with Bishop was laughin' at everything he pulled—that is, he thought she was laughin'. The fact was that she was snatchin' the chance to show more o' them teeth. They wasn't no use showin' 'em to me; so I didn't get laughs from her on my stuff, only when he or some other stranger was round. And if my stuff wasn't funnier than Bishop's I'll lay down my life for Austria.

As a general rule, I don't think a man is justified in interferin' with other people's hymeneal intentions, but it's different when the said intentions is goin' to make your own home a hell.

It was up to me to institute proceedin's that would check the flight o' these two cooin' doves before their wings took 'em to Crown Point in a yellow flivver.

And I seen my duty all the more clear when the pair come home from the ball game the day after Bessie's arrival, and not only told me that the White Sox got another trimmin' but laughed when they said it.

"Well, Bishop," I says when we set down to supper, "how many six-reelers are you turnin' out a day?"

"About one every two weeks is the limit," says Bishop.

"I'll bet it is," I says. "And who are you workin' for now?"

"The Western Film Corporation," he says. "But I'm goin' to quit 'em the first o' the month."

"What for?" I ast him.

"Better offer from the Criterion," he says.

"Better'n ten thousand a year?" says I.

"Sure!" he says.

"Twenty dollars better?" I says.

He blushed and the Wife sunk my shin with a patent-leather torpedo. Then Bishop says:

"The raise I'm gettin' would make twenty dollars look sick."

"If you'd give it to me," I says, "I'd try and nurse it back to health."

After supper the Missus called me out in the kitchen to bawl me out.

"It's rough stuff to embarrass a guest," she says.

"He's always embarrassed," says I. "But you admit now, don't you, that I was tellin' the truth about him touchin' me?"

"Yes," she says.

"Well," says I, "if he's so soiled with money, why don't he pay a little puny debt?"

"He's probably forgot it," says she.

"Did he look like he'd forgot it?" I ast her. And she had no come-back.

But when my Missus can overlook a guy stingin' me for legal tender, it means he's in pretty strong with her. And I couldn't count on no help from her, even if Bishop was a murderer, so long as Bess wanted him.

The next mornin', just to amuse myself, I called up the Criterion people and ast them if they was goin' to hire a scenario writer name Elmer Bishop.

"Never heard of him," was what they told me.

So I called up the Western.

"Elmer Bishop?" they says. "He ain't no scenario writer. He's what we call an extra. He plays small parts sometimes."

"And what pay do them extras drag down?" I ast.

"Five dollars a day, but nothin' when they don't work," was the thrillin' response.

My first idea was to slip this dope to the Wife and Bess both. But what'd be the use? They wouldn't believe it even if they called up and found out for themself; and if they did believe it, Bessie'd say a man's pay didn't make no difference where true love was concerned, and the Missus would take her part, and they'd cry a little, and wind up by sendin' for Bishop and a minister to make sure o' the ceremony comin' off before Bishop lost his five-dollar job and croaked himself.

Then I thought o' forbiddin' him the hospitality o' my abode. But that'd be just as useless. They'd meet somewheres else, and if I threatened to lock Bess out, the Wife'd come back with a counter-proposition to not give me no more stewed beets or banana soufflés. Besides that, strong-arm methods don't never kill sweet love, but act just the opposite and make the infected parties more set on gettin' each other. This here case was somethin' delicate, and if a man didn't handle it exactly right you wouldn't never get over bein' sorry.

So, instead o' me quarrelin' with the Wife and Bess, and raisin' a fuss at Bishop spendin' eight evenin's a week with us, I kept my clam closed and tried to be pleasant, even when I'd win a hand o' rummy and see this guy carelessly lose a few of his remainin' face cards under the table.

We had an awful spell o' heat in July and it wasn't no fun playin' cards or goin' to pitcher shows, or nothin'. Saturday afternoons and Sundays, I and the Missus would go over to the lake and splash. Bess only went with us a couple o' times; that was because she couldn't get Bishop to come along. He'd always say he was busy, or he had a cold and was afraid o' makin' it worse. So far as I was concerned, I managed to enjoy my baths just as much with them two stayin' away. The sight o' Bessie in a bathin' suit crabbed the exhilaratin' effects o' the swim. When she stood up in the water the minnows must of thought two people was still-fishin'.

It was one night at supper, after Bessie'd been with us about a month, when the idear come to me. Bishop was there, and I'd been lookin' at he and Bess, and wonderin' what they'd seen in each other. The Missus ast 'em if they was goin' out some place.

"No," says Bessie. "It's too hot and they ain't no place to go."

"They's lots o' places to go," says the Wife. "For one thing, they're havin' grand opera out to Ravinia Park."

"I wouldn't give a nickel to see a grand opera," says Bess, "unless it was *Ada,* that Elmer took us to last winter."

So they went on talkin' about somethin' else. I don't know what, because the minute she mentioned *Ada* I was all set.

I guess maybe I'd better tell you a little about this here opera, so's you'll see how it helped me out. A fella named Gus Verdi wrote it, and the scenes is laid along the Illinois Central, round Memphis and Cairo. Ada's a big wench, with a pretty voice, and she's the hired girl in the mayor's family. The mayor's daughter gets stuck on a fat little tenor that you can't pronounce and that should of had a lawn mower ran over his chin. The tenor likes the colored girl better than the mayor's daughter, and the mayor's daughter tries every way she can think of to bust it up and grab off the tenor for herself; but nothin' doin'! Finally the mayor has the tenor pinched for keepin' open after one o'clock, and the law's pretty strict; so, instead o' just finin' him, they lock him up in a safety-deposit vault. Well, the wench is down in the vault, too, dustin' off the papers and cleanin' the silver, and they don't know she's there; so the two o' them's locked up together and can't get out. And when they can't get away and haven't got nobody else to look at or talk to, they get so's they hate each other; and finally they can't stand it no longer and they both die. They's pretty music in it, but if old Gus had of seen the men that was goin' to be in the show he'd of laid the scenes in Beardstown instead o' Memphis.

Well, do you get the idear? If the mayor's daughter had of been smart, instead o' tryin' to keep the tenor and Ada from bein' with each other she'd of locked 'em up together a long while ago, and, first thing you know, they'd of been sick o' one another; and just before they died she could of let 'em out and had the tenor for herself without no argument.

And the same thing would work with Bishop and Bess. In all the time o' their mutual courtship they hadn't been together for more'n five or six hours at a time, and never where one o' them couldn't make a quick duck when they got tired. Make 'em stick round with each other for a day, or for two days, without no chance to separate, and it was a cinch that the alarm clock would break in on Love's Young Dream.

But, for some reason or other, I didn't have no safety-deposit vault and they wasn't no room in the flat that they couldn't get out of by jumpin' from the window.

How was I goin' to work it? I thought and thought; and figured and figured; and it wasn't till after I'd went to bed that the solution come.

A boat trip to St. Joe! I and the Missus and the two love birds. And I'd see to it that the chaperons kept their distance and let Nature take its course. We'd go over some Saturday afternoon and come back the next night. That'd give 'em eight or nine hours Saturday and from twelve to sixteen hours Sunday to get really acquainted with each other. And if they was still on speakin' terms at the end o' that time I'd pass up the case as incurable.

You see, I had it doped that Bishop was afraid o' water or else he wouldn't of turned down all our swimmin' parties. I wouldn't leave him a chance to duck out o' this because I wouldn't tell nobody where we was goin'. It'd be a surprise trip. And they was a good chance that they'd both be sick if it was the least bit rough, and that'd help a lot. I thought of Milwaukee first, but picked St. Joe because it's dry. A man might stand for Bess a whole day and more if he was a little blear-eyed from Milwaukee's favorite food.

The trip would cost me some money, but it was an investment with a good chance o' big returns. I'd of been willin' to take 'em to Palm Beach for a month if that'd been the only way to save my home.

When Bishop blew in the next evenin' I pulled it on 'em.

"Bishop," I says, "a man that does as much brain work as you ought to get more recreation."

"I guess I do work too hard," he says modestly.

"I should think," I says, "that you'd give yourself Saturday afternoons and Sundays off."

"I do, in summer," he says.

"That's good," I says. "I was thinkin' about givin' a little party this comin' week-end; and, o' course, I wanted you to be in on it."

The two girls got all excited.

"Party!" says the Missus. "What kind of a party?"

"Well," I says, "I was thinkin' about takin' you and Bishop and Bess out o' town for a little trip."

"Where to?" ast the Wife.

"That's a secret," I says. "You won't know where we're goin' till we start. All I'll tell you is that we'll be gone from Saturday afternoon till Monday mornin'."

"Oh, how grand!" says Bessie. "And think how romantic it'll be, not knowin' where we're headed!"

"I don't know if I can get away or not," says Bishop.

"I pay all expenses," says I.

"Oh, Elmer, you've just got to go!" says Bess.

"The trip's off if you don't," I says.

"If you don't say yes I'll never speak to you again," says Bessie.

For a minute I hoped he wouldn't say yes; but he did. Then I told 'em that the start would be from our house at a quarter to one Saturday, and to pack up their sporty clothes. The rest o' the evenin' was spent in them tryin' to guess where we was goin'. It got 'em nothin', because I wouldn't say aye, yes or no to none o' their guesses.

When I and the Missus was alone, she says:

"Well, what's the idear?"

"No idear at all," I says, "except that our honeymoon trip to Palm Beach was a flivver and I feel like as if I ought to make up to you for it. And besides that, Bessie's our guest and I ought to do somethin' nice for she and her friend."

"I'd think you must of been drinkin' if I didn't know better," she says.

"You never do give me credit for nothin'," says I. "To tell the truth, I'm kind of ashamed o' myself for the way I been actin' to'rd Bishop and Bess; but I'm willin' to make amends before it's too late. If Bishop's goin' to be one o' the family I and him should ought to be good friends."

"That's the way I like to hear you talk," says the Wife.

"But remember," I says, "this trip ain't only for their benefit, but for our'n too. And from the minute we start till we get home us two'll pal round together just like we was alone. We don't want them buttin' in on us and we don't want to be buttin' in on them."

"That suits me fine!" says she. "And now maybe you'll tell me where we're goin'."

"You promise not to tell?" I ast her.

"Sure!" she says.

"Well," I says, "that's one promise you'll keep."

And I buried my good ear in the feathers.

At twenty minutes to two, Saturday afternoon, I landed my entire party at the dock, foot o' Wabash Avenue.

"Goody!" says Bess. "We're goin' acrost the lake."

"If the boat stays up."

"I don't know if I ought to go or not," says Bishop. "I'd ought to be where I can keep in touch with the Criterion people."

"They got a wireless aboard," I says.

"Yes," says Bishop; "but they wouldn't know where to reach me."

"You got time to phone 'em before we sail," says I.

"No, he hasn't," says Bessie. "He ain't goin' to take no chance o' missin' this boat. He can send 'em a wireless after we start."

So that settled Bishop, and he had to walk up the gangplank with the rest of us. He looked just as pleased as if they'd lost his laundry.

I checked the baggage and sent the three o' them up on deck, sayin' I'd join 'em later. Then I ast a boy where the bar was.

"Right in there," he says, pointin'. "But you can't get nothin' till we're three miles out."

So I went back to the gangplank and started off the boat. A man about four years old, with an addin' machine in his hand, stopped me.

"Are you goin' to make the trip?" he ast me.

"What do you think I'm on here for—to borrow a match?" says I.

"Well," he says, "you can't get off."

"You're cross!" I says. "I bet your milk don't agree with you."

I started past him again, but he got in front o' me.

"You can get off, o' course," he says; "but you can't get back on. That's the rules."

"What sense is they in that?" I ast him.

"If I let people off, and on again, my count would get mixed up," he says.

"Who are you?" says I.

"I'm the government checker," he says.

"Chess?" says I. "And you count all the people that gets on?"

"That's me," he says.

"How many's on now?" I ast him.

"Eight hundred-odd," he says.

"I ast you for the number, not the description," I says. "How many's the limit?" I ast him.

"Thirteen hundred," he says.

"And would the boat sink if they was more'n that?" says I.

"I don't know if it would or wouldn't," he says, "but that's all the law allows."

For a minute I felt like offerin' him a lump sum to let seven or eight hundred more on the boat and be sure that she went down; meantime I'd be over gettin' a drink. But then I happened to think that the Missus would be among those lost; and though a man might do a whole lot better the second time, the chances was that he'd do a whole lot worse. So I passed up the idear and stayed aboard, prayin' for the time when we'd be three miles out on Lake Michigan.

It was the shortest three miles you ever seen. We hadn't got out past the Municipal Pier when I seen a steady influx goin' past the engine-room and into the great beyond. I followed 'em and got what I was after. Then I went up on deck, lookin' for my guests.

I found 'em standin' in front o' one o' the lifeboats.

"Why don't you get comfortable?" I says to Bishop. "Why don't you get chairs and enjoy the breeze?"

"That's what I been tellin' 'em," says the Missus; "but Mr. Bishop acts like he was married to this spot."

"I'm only thinkin' of your wife and Bessie," says Bishop. "If anything happened, I'd want 'em to be near a lifeboat."

"Nothin's goin' to happen," I says. "They hasn't been a wreck on this lake for over a month. And this here boat, the *City o' Benton Harbor,* ain't never sank in her life."

"No," says Bishop; "and the *Chicora* and *Eastland* never sank till they sunk."

"The boats that sinks," I says, "is the boats that's overloaded. I was talkin' to the government checker-player down-stairs and he tells me that you put thirteen hundred on this boat and she's perfectly safe; and they's only eight hundred aboard now."

"Then why do they have the lifeboats?" ast Bishop.

"So's you can go back if you get tired o' the trip," I says.

"I ought to be back now," says Bishop, "where the firm can reach me."

"We ain't more'n two miles out," I says. "If your firm's any good they'll drag the bottom farther out than this. Besides," I says, "if trouble comes the lifeboats would handle us."

"Yes," says Bishop; "but it's women and children rst."

"Sure!" I says. "That's the proper order for drownin'. The world couldn't struggle along without us ten-thousand-dollar scenario writers."

"They couldn't be no trouble on such a lovely day as this," says Bess.

"That's where you make a big mistake," I

says. "That shows you don't know nothin' about the history o' Lake Michigan."

"What do you mean?" ast Bishop.

"All the wrecks that's took place on this lake," I says, "has happened in calm weather like to-day. It's just three years ago this July," I says, "when the *City of Ypsilanti* left Grand Haven with about as many passengers as we got to-day. The lake was just like a billiard table and no thought o' danger. Well, it seems like they's a submerged water oak about three miles from shore that you're supposed to steer round it. But this pilot hadn't never made the trip before, and, besides that, he'd been drinkin' pretty heavy; so what does he do but run right plump into the tree, and the boat turned a turtle and all the passengers was lost except a tailor named Swanson."

"But that was just an unreliable officer," says Bessie. "He must of been crazy."

"Crazy!" says I. "They wouldn't nobody work on these boats unless they was crazy. It's bound to get 'em."

186

"I hope we got a reliable pilot to-day," says Bishop.

"He's only just a kid," I says; "and I noticed him staggerin' when he come aboard. But, anyway, you couldn't ask for a better bottom than they is right along in here; nice clean sand and hardly any weeds."

"What time do we get to St. Joe?" ast Bishop.

"About seven if we don't run into a squall," I says.

Then I and the Wife left 'em and went round to another part o' the deck and run into squalls of all nationalities. Their mothers had made a big mistake in bringin' 'em, because you could tell from their faces and hands that they didn't have no use for water.

"They all look just alike," says the Missus. "I don't see how the different mothers can tell which is their baby."

"It's fifty-fifty," I says. "The babies don't look no more alike than the mothers. The mothers is all named Jennie, and all perfect cubes and fond of apples, and ought to go to a dentist. Besides," I says, "suppose they did get mixed up and swap kids, none o' the parties concerned would have reasons to gloat. And the babies certainly couldn't look no more miserable under different auspices than they do now."

We walked all round the deck, threadin' our way among the banana peelin's, and lookin' our shipmates over.

"Pick out somebody you think you'd like to meet," I told the Wife, "and I'll see if I can arrange it."

"Thanks," she says; "but I'll try and not get lonesome, with my husband and my sister and my sister's beau along."

"It's nice for you to say it," says I; "but you want to remember that we're leavin' Bess and Bishop to themself, and that leaves you and I to ourself, and they ain't no two people in the world that can spend two days alone together without gettin' bored stiff. Besides, you don't want to never overlook a chance to meet high-class people."

"When I get desperately anxious to meet high-class people," she says, "I'll be sure and pick out the Saturday afternoon boat from Chicago to St. Joe."

"You can't judge people by their looks," says I. "You haven't heard 'em talk."

"No; and couldn't understand 'em if I did," she says.

"I'll bet some o' them's just as bright as we are," I says.

"I'm not lookin' for bright companionship," she says. "I want a change."

"That's just like I told you," says I. "You're bound to get tired o' one person, no matter how much they sparkle, if you live with 'em long enough."

We left the deck and went down-stairs. They was two or three people peerin' in the engine-room and the Missus made me stop there a minute.

"What for?" I ast her.

"I want to see how it works," she says.

"Well," says I, when we'd started on again, "I can drop my insurance now."

"Why?" says the Missus.

"I don't never need to worry about you starvin'," I says. "With the knowledge you just picked up there, I bet you could easy land a job as engineer on one o' these boats."

"I'd do about as good as you would at it," she says.

"Sure; because I didn't study it," I says. "What makes the boat run?" I ast her.

"Why, the wheel," she says.

"And who runs the wheel?" I ast her.

"The pilot," says she.

"And what does the engineer do?" I says.

"Why, I suppose he keeps the fire burnin'," she says.

"But in weather like this what do they want of a fire?"

"I suppose it gets colder out in the middle o' the lake," she says.

"No," says I; "but on Saturdays they got to keep a fire goin' to heat the babies' bottles."

We went in the room next to the bar. A boy set at the piano playin' *Sweet Cider Time in Moonshine Valley* and some Hawaiian native melodies composed by a Hungarian waiter that was too proud to fight. Three or four couple was dancin', but none o' them was wrynecked enough to get the proper pose. The girls looked pretty good and was probably members o' the Four Hundred employed in the Fair. The boys would of been handsomer if the laundry hadn't failed to bring back their other shirt in time.

A big guy in a uniform come by and went into the next room. "Is that the captain?" ast the Wife.

"No," I says, "that's the steward."

"And what does he do?" she ast me.

"He hangs round the bar," I says, "and looks after the stews."

"Have they really got a bar?" she says.

"I'll find out for sure if you'll wait here a

minute," says I, and led her to a chair where she could watch 'em wrestle.

In the other room I stood next to a Greek that charged ten cents on Sundays and holidays. He was all lit up like the Municipal Pier.

"Enjoyin' the trip?" I ast him.

"Too rough; too rough!" he says, only I don't do the dialect very good.

"I bet you never got that shine at your own stand," says I.

"Too hot to work!" says he. "I don't have to work. I got the mon'."

"Yes," I says; "and the bun."

A little way off from us was four other political enemies o' J. Frank Hanly, tellin' my Greek friend in tonsorial tones that if he didn't like his Uncle Sammy he knowed what he could do.

"Don't you like your Uncle Sammy?" I ast him.

"I don't have to work," he says. "I got the mon'."

"Then why don't you take them boys' advice," I says, "and go back to your home o'er the sea?"

"Too rough; too rough!" he says; and in the twenty minutes I stood there with him, findin' out whether they was really a bar, he didn't say nothin' except that he had the mon', and he didn't have to work, and somethin' was too rough.

I and the Missus went back up on deck. I steered for the end o' the boat that was farthest from where we'd left Bess and Bishop, but they'd began to get restless, and we run into them takin' a walk.

"Where you been?" ast Bessie.

"Down watchin' 'em dance," says the Missus.

"Is they a place to dance aboard?" ast Bishop.

But I didn't want 'em to dance, because that'd be an excuse not to say nothin' to each other for a w'ile. So I says:

"They's a place, all right; but five or six

couple's already on the floor, and when you get more'n that trottin' round at once it's li'ble to rock the boat and be disastrous."

I took the Wife's arm and started to move on.

"Where you goin'?" says Bishop.

"Just for a stroll round the decks," says I.

"We'll go along," he says.

I seen the treatment was beginnin' to work. "Nothin' doin'!" I says. "This is one of our semi-annual honeymoons and we can't use no outside help."

A few minutes before we hit St. Joe we seen 'em again, settin' down below, afraid to dance and entirely out o' conversation. They was havin' just as good a time as Jennie's babies.

"We're pretty near in," I says, "and 'twas one o' the smoothest crossin's I ever made."

"They couldn't nobody get sick in weather like this," says Bess.

"No," I says, "but you take a smooth Saturday afternoon and it generally always means a rough Sunday night."

"Ain't they no railroad between here and Chi?" ast Bishop.

"Not direct," I says. "You have to go to Lansing and then cut across to Fort Wayne. If you make good connections you can do it in a day and two nights, but most o' the way is through the copper ranges and the trains keeps gettin' later and later, and when they try to make up time they generally always slip offen the track and spill their contents."

"If it looks like a storm to-morrow night," says Bess, "we might wait over and go home Monday."

That idear scared Bishop more'n the thought of a wreck.

"Oh, no!" he says. "I got to be back on the job Monday mornin'."

"If it's as rough as I think it's goin' to be," says I, "you won't feel like rippin' off no scenarios Monday."

We landed and walked up the highest hill in Michigan to the hotel. I noticed that Miss Bessie carried her own suit-case.

"Well," I says, "I suppose you two kids would rather eat your supper by yourself, and I and the Missus will set at another table."

"No, no!" says Bess. "It'll be pleasanter to all eat together."

So for about half an hour we had 'em with us; and they'd of stuck the rest o' the evenin' if I'd gave 'em a chance.

"What about a little game o' cards?" says Bishop, when we was through eatin'.

"It's mighty nice o' you to suggest it," I says; "but I know you're only doin' it for my sake and the Wife's. We'll find some way to amuse ourself, and you and Bess can take a stroll down on the beach."

"The wind made me sleepy," says Bishop. "I believe I'll go up to my room and turn in."

"The rooms is not ready," I says. "The clerk'll let us know as soon as we can have 'em."

But he didn't take my word; and when he'd talked to the clerk himself, and found out that he could have his room right away, they wasn't no arguin' with him. Off he went to bed at eight P. M., leavin' the Missus and I to entertain the Belle o' Wabash.

Sunday mornin' I added to my investment by hirin' a flivver to take us out to the Edgewater Club.

"Now," I says, "we'll rent some bathin' suits and cool off."

"I don't dast go in," says Bishop. "I'd take more cold. I'll watch the rest o' you."

Well, I didn't care whether he went in or not, the water bein' too shallow along there to drownd him; but I did want him to watch the rest of us—one in particular.

The suit they gave her was an Annette. I wouldn't make no attempt to describe what she looked like in it, unless it'd be a capital Y that had got turned upside down. She didn't have no displacement and she could of stayed in all day without the lake ever findin' out she was there.

But I cut the film short so's I could get 'em back to the hotel and leave the pair together again.

"You're goin' to have all the rest o' the day to yourself," I told 'em. "We won't eat dinner with you. I and the Missus will just disappear and meet you here in the hotel at seven o'clock to-night."

"Where are you goin'?" ast Bishop.

"Never you mind," I says.

"Maybe we'd like to go along with you," he says.

"Yes, you would!" says I. "Remember, boy, I was in love once myself, and I know I didn't want no third parties hangin' round."

"But what can we do all day in this burg?" he says.

"They's plenty to do," I says. "You can go over there and set on them benches and watch the interurbans come in from South Bend and Niles, or you can hire a boat and go out for a sail, or you can fish for tarpons; or you can take a trolley over to Benton Har-

bor; or you can set on the beach and spoon.
Nobody minds here—only be sure you don't
set in somebody's lunch basket, because they
say a garlic stain's almost impossible to get
out. And they's another thing you might do,"
I says: "this town's one o' these here Gretna
Greens. You can get a marriage license in any
delicatessen and the street-car conductors is au-
thorized to perform the ceremony."

They didn't blush when I pulled that; they
turned pale, both o' them, and I seen that I
was goin' to win, sure.

"Come on!" I says to the Missus. "We must
be on our way."

We left 'em before they could stop us and
walked acrost the street and along through the
park.

"Where are we headed?" ast the Wife.

"I don't know," I says; "but I don't want
to spoil their good time."

"I don't believe they're havin' a good time,"
she says.

"How could they help it?" says I. "When

two true lovers is left alone together, what more could they ast for?"

"They's somethin' wrong with 'em," says the Missus. "They act like they was mad at each other. And Bess told me when we was out to the Edgewater Club that she wished we was home."

"That's a fine way for her to talk," I says, "when I'm tryin' to show her a good time!"

"And I overheard Elmer," says the Missus, "askin' one o' the bell boys where he could get somethin' to drink; and the bell boy ast him what kind of a drink, and he says, whisky or poison—it didn't make no difference."

"If I was sure he'd take the poison I'd try to get it for him," I says.

On the grass and the benches in the park we seen some o' the gang that'd came over on the boat with us. They looked like they'd laid there all night and the kids was cryin' louder'n ever. Besides them we seen dozens o' young couples that was still on speakin' terms, because they'd only been together an hour or two.

THE WATER CURE

The girls was wearin' nice, clean, white dresses and white shoes, and was all prettied up. They seemed to be havin' the time o' their life. And by four o'clock in the afternoon their fingers would be stuck together with crackerjack and their dresses decorated with chocolate sirup, and their escorts talkin' to 'em like a section boss to a gang o' hunkies.

We wandered round till dinner-time, and then dropped into a little restaurant where they give you a whole meal for thirty-five cents and make a profit of thirty-five cents. When we'd staggered out under the weight o' this repast, a street-car was standin' there that said it would take us to the House o' David.

"Come on!" I says, and led the Missus aboard.

"Where to?" she ast me.

"I don't know," I says; "but it sounds like a road house."

It was even better'n that. You couldn't get nothin' to drink, but they was plenty to see and hear—band concerts, male and female;

movin' pitchers; a zoo; a bowlin' alley; and more funny-lookin' people than I ever seen in an amusement park before.

It ain't a regular amusement park, but fifty-fifty between that and a kind of religious sex that calls themself the Holy Roller Skaters or somethin'. All the men that was old enough to keep a beard had one; and for a minute I thought we'd bumped into the summer home o' the people that took part in *Ada*.

They wouldn't nobody of ever mistook the women for *Follies* chorus girls. They looked like they was havin' a prize contest to see which could dress the homeliest; and if I'd been one o' the judges I'd of split the first prize as many ways as they was women.

"I'm goin' to talk to some o' these people," I told the Wife.

"What for?" she says.

"Well, for one thing," I says, "I been talkin' to one person so long I'm tired of it; and, for another thing, I want to find out what the idear o' the whole concern is."

THE WATER CURE

So we walked up to one o' the most flourishin' beards and I braced him.

"Who owns this joint?" I says.

"All who have the faith," he says.

"What do they charge a man to join?" I ast him.

"Many's called and few chosen," he says.

"How long have you been here?" I ast him.

"Prove all things and hold fast to what's good," he says. "Why don't you get some of our books and study 'em?"

He led us over to where they had the books and I looked at some o' them. One was the *Flyin' Roll,* and another was the *Livin' Roll o' Life,* and another was the *Rollin' Ball o' Fire.*

"If you had some books about coffee you could make a breakfast on 'em," I says.

Well, we stuck round there till pretty near six o'clock and talked to a lot o' different ones and ast 'em all kinds o' questions; and they answered 'em all with verses from Scripture that had nothin' to do with what we'd ast.

"We got a lot of information," says the Wife on the way back to St. Joe. "We don't know no more about 'em now than before we come."

"We know their politics," I says.

"How?" she ast me.

"From the looks of 'em," I says. "They're unanimous for Hughes."

We found Bess all alone, settin' in the lobby o' the hotel.

"Where's your honey man?" I ast her.

She turned up her nose.

"Don't call him my honey man or my anything else," she says.

"Why, what's the matter?" ast the Missus.

"Nothin' at all's the matter," she says.

"Maybe just a lovers' quarrel," says I.

"No, and no lovers' quarrel, neither," says Bess. "They couldn't be no lovers' quarrel, because they ain't no lovers."

"You had me fooled, then," I says. "I'd of swore that you and Bishop was just like that."

"You made a big mistake," says Bessie. "I

never cared nothin' for him and he never cared nothin' for me, because he's incapable o' carin' for anything—only himself."

"Why, Bess," says the Missus, "you told me just yesterday mornin' that you was practically engaged!"

"I don't care what I told you," she says; "but I'm tellin' you somethin' now: I don't never want to hear of him or see him again. And you'll do me a favor if you'll drop the subject."

"But where is he?" I ast her.

"I don't know and I don't care!" she says.

"But I got to find him," I says. "He's my guest."

"You can have him," she says.

I found him up in his room. The bell boy had got him somethin', and it wasn't poison, neither. At least I haven't never died of it.

"Well, Bishop," I says, "finish it up and come down-stairs. Bess and the Wife'll want some supper."

"You'll have to excuse me," he says. "I don't feel like eatin' a thing."

"But you can come down and set with us,"
I says. "Bess will be sore if you don't."

"Listen here!" he says. "You've took too
much for granted. They's nothin' between
your sister-in-law and I. If you've set your
heart on us bein' somethin' more'n friends, I'm
sorry. But they's not a chance."

"Bishop," I says, "this is a blow to me. It
comes like a shock."

And to keep myself from faintin' I took the
bottle from his dresser and completed its ruin.

"You won't even come down and set with
us?" I says.

"No," says Bishop. "And, if you don't
mind, you can give me my ticket back home
and I'll stroll down to the dock and meet you
on the boat."

"Here's your ticket," says I.

"And where am I goin' to sleep?" he says.

"Well," I says, "I'll get you a stateroom
if you really want it; but it's goin' to be a bad
night, and if you was in one o' them berths,

and somethin' happened, you wouldn't have a chance in the world!"

"You ain't goin' to have no berth, yourself?" he ast me.

"I should say not!" I says. "I'm goin' to get me a chair and sleep in the water-tight compartments."

Boys, my prophecy come true. They was more roll on old Lake Michigan that night than in all them books up to the Holy Roller Skaters' park. And if the boat was filled to capacity just thirteen hundred of us was fatally ill.

I don't think it was the rollin' that got me. It was one glimpse of all the Jennies and their offsprings, and the wealthy Greek shoe shiners, and the millionaire truck drivers, and the heiresses from the Lace Department—layin' hither and thither in the cabins and on the decks, breathin' their last. And how they must of felt to think that all their outlay for crackerjack and apples was a total loss!

But Bishop wasn't sick. I searched the boat from the back to the stern and he wasn't aboard. I guess probably he found out some way that they was such an institution as the Père Marquette, which gets into Chicago without touchin' them perilous copper ranges. But whether he arrived safe or not I don't know, because I've never saw him from that day to this, and I've lived happy ever afterward.

And my investment, amountin' all told to just about what he owes me, turned out even better than I'd hoped for. Bess went back to Wabash that Monday afternoon.

At supper Monday night, which was the first meal the Missus could face, she says:

"I haven't got it figured out yet. Bess swears they didn't have no quarrel; but I'll take an oath they was in love with each other. What could of happened?"

"I know what happened," I says. "They got acquainted!"

THREE WITHOUT, DOUBLED

I

THEY ain't no immediate chance o' you gettin' ast out to our house to dinner—not w'ile round steak and General Motors is sellin' at the same price and common dog biscuit's ten cents a loaf. But you might have nothin' decent to do some evenin' and happen to drop in on the Missus and I for a call; so I feel like I ought to give you a little warnin' in case that comes off.

You know they's lots o' words that's called fightin' words. Some o' them starts a brawl, no matter who they're spoke to. You can't call nobody a liar without expectin' to lose a couple o' milk teeth—that is, if the party addressed has got somethin' besides lemon juice in his veins and ain't had the misfortune to fall asleep on the Panhandle tracks and be separated from his most prominent legs and arms. Then they's terms that don't hit you so much yourself, but reflects on your ancestors and prodigies, and you're supposed to resent 'em for the sake of honor and fix the speaker's map so as when he goes home his wife'll say: "Oh, kiddies! Come and look at the rainbow!"

Then they's other words and terms that you can call 'em to somebody and not get no rise; but call 'em to somebody else and the insurance companies could hold out on your widow by claimin' it was suicide. For instance, they's young Harold Greiner, one o' the bookkeepers down to the office. I could tell him he was an A. P. A., with a few adjectives, and he'd just smile and say: "Quit your flirtin'!" But I wouldn't never try that expression on Dan Cahill, the elevator starter, without bein' well out of his earshots. And I don't know what it means, at that.

Well, if you do come out to the house they's a term that you want to lay off of when the Missus is in the room. Don't say: "San Susie!"

THREE WITHOUT, DOUBLED

It sounds harmless enough, don't it? They ain't nothin' to it even when it's transferred over from the Latin, "Without no cares." But just leave her hear it mentioned and watch her grab the two deadliest weapons that's within reach, one to use on you or whoever said it, and the other on me, on general principles.

You think I'm stringin' you, and I admit you got cause—that is, till you've heard the details of our latest plunge in the cesspools o' Society.

II

It was a Friday evenin' about three weeks ago when I come home and found the Wife quaverin' with excitement.

"Who do you think called up?" she ast me.

"I got no idear," I says.

"Guess!" says she.

So I had to guess.

"Josephus Daniels," I says. "Or Henry Ford. Or maybe it was that guy with the scar on his lip that you thought was smilin' at you the other day."

"You couldn't never guess," she says. "It was Mrs. Messenger."

"Which one?" I ast her. "You can't mean Mrs. A. D. T. Messenger."

"If you're so cute I won't tell you nothin' about it," says she.

"Don't make no rash threats," I says. "You're goin' to tell me some time and they's no use makin' yourself sick by tryin' to hold it in."

"You know very well what Mrs. Messenger I mean," she says. "It was Mrs. Robert Messenger that's husband owns this buildin' and the one at the corner, where they live at."

"Haven't you paid the rent?" I says.

"Do you think a woman like Mrs. Messenger would be buttin' into her husband's business?" says the Missus.

"I don't know what kind of a woman Mrs. Messenger is," I says. "But if I owned these here apartments and somebody fell behind in their rent, I wouldn't be surprised to see the owner's wife goin' right over to their flat and takin' it out o' their trousers pocket."

"Well," says the Wife, "we don't owe them no rent and that wasn't what she called up about. It wasn't no business call."

"Go ahead and spill it," I says. "My heart's weak."

"Well," she says, "I was just gettin' through with the lunch dishes and the phone rang."

"I bet you wondered who it was," says I.

"I thought it was Mrs. Hatch or somebody," says the Wife. "So I run to the phone and it was Mrs. Messenger. So the first thing she says was to explain who she was—just like I didn't know. And the next thing she ast was did I play bridge."

"And what did you tell her?" says I.

"What do you think I'd tell her?" says the Missus. "I told her yes."

"Wasn't you triflin' a little with the truth?" I ast her.

"Certainly not!" she says. "Haven't I

played twice over to Hatches'? So then she ast me if my husband played bridge, too. And I told her yes, he did."

"What was the idear?" I says. "You know I didn't never play it in my life."

"I don't know no such a thing," she says. "For all as I know, you may play all day down to the office."

"No," I says; "we spend all our time down there playin' post-office with the scrubwomen."

"Well, anyway, I told her you did," says the Missus. "Don't you see they wasn't nothin' else I could tell her, because if I told her you didn't, that would of ended it."

"Ended what?" I says.

"We wouldn't of been ast to the party," says the Missus.

"Who told you they was goin' to be a party?" I says.

"I don't have to be told everything," says the Missus. "I got brains enough to know that Mrs. Messenger ain't callin' me up and astin' me do we play bridge just because she's got a headache or feels lonesome or somethin'. But it ain't only one party after all, and that's the best part of it. She ast us if we'd care to join the club."

"What club?" says I.

"Mrs. Messenger's club, the San Susie Club," says the Missus. "You've heard me speak about it a hundred times, and it's been mentioned in the papers once or twice, too— once, anyway, when the members give away them Christmas dinners last year."

"We can get into the papers," I says, "without givin' away no Christmas dinners."

"Who wants to get into the papers?" says the Wife. "I don't care nothin' about that."

"No," I says; "I suppose if a reporter come out here and ast for your pitcher to stick in the society columns, you'd pick up the carvin' knife and run him ragged."

"I'd be polite to him, at least," she says.

"Yes," says I; "it wouldn't pay to treat him rude; it'd even be justifiable to lock him in w'ile you was lookin' for the pitcher."

"If you'll kindly leave me talk you may find out what I got to say," she says. "I've told you about this club, but I don't suppose you ever paid any attention. It's a club that's made up from people that just lives in this block, twenty o' them altogether; and all but one couple either lives in this buildin' or in the buildin' the Messengers lives in. And they're all nice people, people with real class to them; not no tramps like most o' the ones we been runnin' round with. One o' them's Mr. and Mrs. Arthur Collins that used to live on Sheridan Road and still goes over to parties at some o' the most exclusive homes on the North Side. And they don't have nobody in the club that isn't congenial with each other, but all just a nice crowd o' real people that gets together once a week at one o' the members' houses and have a good time."

"How did these pillows o' Society happen to light on to us?" I ast her.

"Well," she says, "it seems like the Baileys, who belonged to the club, went to California last week to spend the winter. And they had to have a couple to take their place. And Mrs. Messenger says they wouldn't take nobody that didn't live in our block, and her and her husband looked over the list and we was the ones they picked out."

"Probably," I says, "that's because we was the only eligibles that can go out nights on account o' not havin' no children."

"The Pearsons ain't ast," she says, "and they ain't got no children."

"Well," I says, "what's the dues?"

"They ain't no dues," says the Missus. "But once in a w'ile, instead o' playin' bridge, everybody puts in two dollars apiece and have a theater party. But the regular program is for an evenin' o' bridge every Tuesday night, at different members' houses, somebody different actin' as hosts every week. And each couple puts up two dollars, makin' ten dollars for a gent's prize and ten dollars for a lady's. And the prizes is picked out by the lady that happens to be the hostess."

"That's a swell proposition for me," I says. "In the first place they wouldn't be a chance in the world for me to win a prize, because I don't know nothin' about the game. And, in the second place, suppose I had a whole lot o' luck and did win the prize, and come to find out it was a silver mustache cup that I wouldn't have no more use for than another Adam's apple! If they paid in cash they might be somethin' to it."

"If you win a prize you can sell it, can't you?" says the Missus. "Besides, the prizes don't count. It's gettin' in with the right kind o' people that makes the difference."

"Another thing," I says: "When it come our turn to have the party, where would we stick 'em all? We'd have to spread a sheet over the bathtub for one table, and have one couple set on the edges and the other couple toss up for the washbasin and the clothes-hamper. And another two couple'd have to kneel round the bed, and another bunch could stand

218

up round the bureau. That'd leave the dinin'-room table for the fourth set; and for a special treat the remainin' four could play in the parlor."

"We could hire chairs and tables," says the Missus. "We're goin' to have to some time, anyway, when you or I die."

"You don't need to hire no tables for my funeral," I says. "If the pallbearers or the quartet insists on shootin' craps they can use the kitchen floor; or if they want beer and sandwiches you can slip 'em the money to go down to the corner."

"They's no use worryin' about our end of it yet," says the Wife. "We'll be new members and they won't expect us to give no party till everybody else has had their turn."

"I only got one objection left," I says. "How am I goin' to get by at a bridge party when I haven't no idear how many cards to deal?"

"I guess you can learn if I learnt," she says.

"You're always talkin' about what a swell card player you are. And besides, you've played w'ist, and they ain't hardly any difference."

"And the next party is next Tuesday night?" I says.

"Yes," says the Missus, "at Mrs. Garrett's, the best player in the club, and one o' the smartest women in Chicago, Mrs. Messenger says. She lives in the same buildin' with the Messengers. And they's dinner first and then we play bridge all evenin'."

"And maybe," I says, "before the evenin's over, I'll find out what's trumps."

"You'll know all about the game before that," she says. "Right after supper we'll get out the cards and I'll show you."

So right after supper she got out the cards and begun to show me. But about all as I learnt was one thing, and that was that if I died without no insurance, the Missus would stand a better show o' supportin' herself by umpirin' baseball in the National League than by teachin' in a bridge-w'ist university. She knew everything except how much the different suits counted, and how many points was in a game, and what honors meant, and who done the first biddin', and how much to bid on what.

After about an hour of it I says:

"I can see you got this thing mastered, but you're like a whole lot of other people that knows somethin' perfect themselves but can't learn it to nobody else."

"No," she says; "I got to admit that I don't know as much as I thought I did. I didn't have no trouble when I was playin' with Mrs. Hatch and Mrs. Pearson and Mrs. Kramer; but it seems like I forgot all they learnt me."

"It's a crime," I says, "that we should have to pass up this chance to get in right just because we can't play a fool game o' cards. Why don't you call up Mrs. Messenger and suggest that the San Susies switches to pedro or five hundred or rummy, or somethin' that you don't need to take no college course in?"

"You're full o' brilliant idears," says the Missus. "They's only just the one game that

Society plays, and that's bridge. Them other games is jokes."

"I've noticed you always treated 'em that way," I says. "But they wasn't so funny to me when it come time to settle."

"I'll tell you what we'll do," says the Missus: "We'll call up Mr. and Mrs. Hatch and tell 'em to come over here to-morrow night and give us a lesson."

"That'd be sweet," I says, "askin' them to learn us a game so as we could join a club that's right here in their neighborhood, but they ain't even been ast to join it!"

"Why, you rummy!" she says. "We don't have to tell 'em why we want to learn. We'll just say that my two attempts over to their house has got me interested and I and you want to master the game so as we can spend many pleasant evenin's with them; because Mrs. Hatch has told me a hundred times that her and her husband would rather play bridge than eat."

So she called up Mrs. Hatch and sprung it

on her; but it seemed like the Hatches had an engagement for Saturday night, but would be tickled to death to come over Monday evenin' and give us a work-out. After that was fixed we both felt kind of ashamed of ourselves, deceivin' people that was supposed to be our best friends.

"But, anyway," the Missus says, "the Hatches wouldn't never fit in with that crowd. Jim always looks like he'd dressed on the elevated and Mrs. Hatch can't talk about nothin' only shiropody."

On the Saturday I tried to slip one over by buyin' a book called *Auction Bridge,* and I read it all the way home from town and then left it on the car. It was a great book for a man that had learnt the rudderments and wanted to find out how to play the game right. But for me to try and get somethin' out of it was just like as though some kid'd learn the baseball guide by heart in kindeygarden and then ask Hugh Jennin's for the job in centerfield. I did find out one thing from it though:

it says that in every deal one o' the players was a dummy and just laid his cards down and left somebody else play 'em. So when I got home I says:

"We won't need no help from Jim Hatch and his wife. We can just be dummies all the evenin' and they won't nobody know if we're ignorant or not."

"That's impossible, to be dummy all the time," says the Missus.

"Not for me," I says. "I know it'll be tough for you, but you can chew a lot o' gum and you won't mind it so much."

"You don't understand," she says. "The dummy is the pardner o' the party that gets the bid. Suppose one o' the people that was playin' against you got the bid; then the other one'd be dummy and you'd have to play your hand."

"But I don't need to leave 'em have the bid," I says. "I can take it away from 'em."

"And if you take it away from 'em," she says, "then you got the bid yourself, and your pardner's dummy, not you."

THREE WITHOUT, DOUBLED

Well, the Hatches breezed in Monday night and Mrs. Hatch remarked how tickled she was that we was goin' to learn, and what good times we four'd have playin' together. And the Missus and I pretended like we shared her raptures.

"Ain't you never played at all?" she ast me; and I told her no.

"The first thing," she says, "is how much the different suits counts; and then they's the bids. And you got to pay attention to the conventions."

"I'm through with 'em forever," I says, "since they turned down Roosevelt."

Well, we started in and Hatch and the Missus played Mrs. Hatch and I. We kept at it till pretty near midnight, with three or four intermissions so as Hatch could relieve the strain on the ice-box. My w'ist education kept me from bein' much of a flivver when it come to playin' the cards; but, I don't care how bright a guy is, you can't learn everything about biddin' in one evenin', and you can't remember half what you learnt. I don't know what the score was when we got through, but the Hatches done most o' the execution and held most o' the cards, which is their regular habit.

"You'll get along all right," says Mrs. Hatch when they was ready to go. "But, o' course, you can't expect to master a game like bridge in a few hours. You want to keep at it."

"We're goin' to," says the Missus.

"Maybe it'd be a good idear," says Mrs. Hatch, "to play again soon before you forget what we learnt you. Why don't you come over to our house for another session to-morrow night?"

"Let's see; to-morow night?" says the Missus, stallin'. "Why, no, we can't. We got an engagement."

So Mrs. Hatch stood there like she was expectin' to hear what it was.

"We're goin' to a party," says the Wife.

"Oh, tell me about it!" says Mrs. Hatch.

"Well," says the Missus, "it ain't really a

party; it's just a kind of a party; some old friends that's visitin' in town."

"Maybe they'll play bridge with you," says Mrs. Hatch.

"Oh, no," says the Missus, blushin'. "It'll probably be rummy or pedro; or maybe we'll just go to the pitchers."

"Why don't you go over to the Acme?" says Mrs. Hatch. "They got Chaplin in *The Street Sweeper*. We're goin', and we could meet you and all go together."

"N-no," says the Wife. "You see, one of our friends has just lost his wife and I know he wouldn't feel like goin' to see somethin' funny."

"He's already laughed himself sick," I says.

Well, we wouldn't make no date with 'em and they finally blew with the understandin' that we was to go to their house and play some night soon. When they'd went the Missus says:

"I feel like a criminal, deceivin' 'em like that. But I just couldn't tell 'em the truth.

Bertha Hatch is the most jealous thing in the world and it would just about kill her to know that we was in on somethin' good without she and Jim."

"If you hadn't ast 'em over," I says, "we'd of been just as well off and you wouldn't of had to make a perjure out o' yourself."

"What do you mean, we'd of been just as well off?" she says. "They done what we expected of 'em, learnt us the game."

"Yes," I says; "and you could take all I remember o' the lesson and feed it to a gnat and he'd say: 'Hurry up with the soup course!'"

III

Well, Mrs. Garrett had called up to say that the feed before the game would begin at seven bells; so I and the Missus figured on bein' on hand at half past six, so as to get acquainted with some of our fellow club members and know what to call 'em when we wanted the gravy passed or somethin'. But I had trouble with my studs and it wasn't till pretty near twenty minutes to seven that we rung the Garretts' bell. The hired girl let us in and left us standin' in the hall w'ile she went to tell Mrs. Garrett we was there. Pretty soon the girl come back and says she would take our wraps and that Mrs. Garrett would be with us in a few minutes. So we was showed into the livin'-room.

The apartment was on the second floor and looked about twice as big as our'n.

"What do you suppose this costs 'em?" ast the Missus.

"About fifty-five a month," I says.

"You're crazy!" says she. "They got this big livin'-room and two big bedrooms, and a maid's room and a sun parlor, besides their dinin'-room and kitchen and bath. They're lucky if they ain't stuck for seventy."

"I'll bet you!" I says. "I'll bet you it's nearer fifty-five than seventy."

"How much'll you bet?" she says.

"Anything you say," says I.

"Well," she says, "I've got a cinch, and I need a pair o' black silk stockin's. My others has begun to run."

"All right," I says. "A pair o' black silk stockin's to fifty cents cash."

"You're on," she says. "And I'll call up the agent to-morrow and find out."

Well, it must of been pretty near seven o'clock when Mrs. Garrett finally showed up.

"Good evenin'," she says. "I suppose this must be our new members. I'm awfully glad you could come and I'm sorry I wasn't quite ready."

"That's all right," I says. "I'm glad to know they's others has trouble gettin' into their evenin' clo'es. I suppose people that does it often enough finally get to be experts."

"I didn't have no trouble," says Mrs. Garrett; "only I didn't expect nobody till seven o'clock. You must of misunderstood me and thought I said half past six."

Then Mr. Garrett come in and shook hands with us, and then the rest o' the folks begun

to arrive and we was introduced to them all.
I didn't catch all their names, only Mr. and
Mrs. Messenger and Mr. and Mrs. Collins and
a Mr. and Mrs. Sparks. Mrs. Garrett says
dinner was ready and I was glad to hear it.

They set me down between Mrs. Messenger
and a lady that I didn't get her name.

"Well," I says to Mrs. Messenger, "now we
know you personally, we can pay the rent direct without botherin' to go to the real-estate
office."

"I'm afraid that wouldn't do," she says.
"Our agent's entitled to his commissions. And
besides, I wouldn't know how much to take or
nothin' about it."

"We pay thirty-five," I says, "and that's all
as you could ast for, seein' we only got the
four rooms and no sun parlor. Thirty-two and
a half would be about the right price."

"You'll have to argue that out with the
agent," she says.

I was kind of expectin' a cocktail; but nothin' doin'. The hired girl brought in some half

sandwiches, made o' toast, with somethin' on 'em that looked like BB shot and tasted like New Year's mornin'.

"Don't we get no liquid refreshments?" I ast Mrs. Messenger.

"No, indeed," she says. "The San Susie's a dry club."

"You should ought to call it the San Sousy, then," says I.

The Missus was settin' next to Mr. Garrett and I could hear 'em talkin' about what a nice neighborhood it was and how they liked their flats. I thought I and the Missus might as well settle our bet then and there, so I spoke to Mr. Garrett acrost the table.

"Mr. Garrett," I says, "w'ile we was waitin' for you and your wife to get dressed, I and the Missus made a little bet, a pair o' silk stockin' against half a buck. I got to pay out two dollars here for the prize and the Missus claims her other stockin's has begun to run; so you might say we're both a little anxious."

"Is it somethin' I can settle?" he ast.

"Yes, sir," I says, "because we was bettin' on the rent you paid for this apartment. The Missus says seventy a month and I says fifty-five."

"I never decide against a lady," he says. "You better buy the stockin's before the others run so far that they can't find their way home."

"If I lose, I lose," says I. "But if you're stuck sixty-five or better, the Missus must of steered me wrong about the number o' rooms you got. I'll pay, though, because I don't never welsh on a bet. So this party's really costin' me two and a half instead o' two."

"Maybe you'll win the prize," says Mr. Garrett.

"They ain't much chance," I says. "I ain't played this game for a long w'ile."

"Why, your wife was just tellin' me you played last night," he says.

"I mean," says I, "that I didn't play for a long w'ile before last night; not for thirty-six years," I says.

Well, when everybody'd got through chokin'

down the shot, they brought in some drowned toadstools, and then some little slices o' beef about the size of a checker, and seven Saratoga chips apiece, and half a dozen string beans. Those that was still able to set up under this load finished up on sliced tomatoes that was caught too young and a nickel's worth of ice-cream and an eyedropper full o' coffee.

"Before I forget it," says Mrs. Collins, w'ile we was staggerin' out o' the dinin'-room, "you're all comin' to my house next Tuesday night."

I was walkin' right behind her.

"And I got a suggestion for you," I says, low enough so as they couldn't nobody else hear: "Throw some o' the prize money into the dinner; and if they's any skimpin' to be done, do it on the prizes."

She didn't say nothin' back, because Mrs. Garrett had started to hand us the little cards that showed where we was to play.

"I suppose I better tell you our rules," she says to me. "Each table plays four deals.

THREE WITHOUT, DOUBLED

Then the winners moves w'ile the losers sets still, except at the first table, where the winners sets still and the losers moves. You change pardners after every four deals. You count fifty for a game and a hundred and fifty for a rubber."

"The way I been playin'," I says, "it was thirty for a game."

"I never heard o' that," she says; but I noticed when we got to playin' that everybody that made thirty points called it a game.

"Don't we see the prizes before we start?" I ast her. "I want to know whether to play my best or not."

"If you win the prize and don't like it," she says, "I guess you can get it exchanged."

"They tell me you're the shark amongst the womenfolks," says I; "so it's a safe bet that you didn't pick out no lady's prize that isn't O. K."

I noticed some o' the other men was slippin' her their ante; so I parted with a two-spot. Then I found where I was to set at. It was

Table Number Three, Couple Number One. My pardner was a strappin' big woman with a name somethin' like Rowley or Phillips. Our opponents was Mrs. Garrett and Mr. Messenger. Mrs. Garrett looked like she'd been livin' on the kind of a meal she'd gave us, and Mr. Messenger could of set in the back seat of a flivver with two regular people without crowdin' nobody. So I says to my pardner:

"Well, pardner, we got 'em outweighed, anyway."

They was two decks o' cards on the table. I grabbed one o' them and begun to deal 'em face up.

"First jack," I says.

"If you don't mind, we'll cut for deal," says Mrs. Garrett.

So we cut the cards and it seemed like the low cut got the deal and that was Mrs. Garrett herself.

"Which deck'll we play with?" I ast.

"Both o' them," says Mrs. Garrett. "Mr. Messenger'll make them red ones for you."

THREE WITHOUT, DOUBLED

"Make 'em!" I says. "Well, Messenger, I didn't know you was a card factory."

Messenger laughed; but the two ladies didn't get it. Mrs. Garrett dealt and it was her turn to bid.

"One without," she says.

"I'd feel better if I had one within," says I.

"Are you goin' to bid or not?" she ast me.

"I thought it was the dealer's turn first," I says.

"I've made my bid," she says. "I bid one without."

"One without lookin', or what?" I says.

"One no trump, if I got to explain it," she says.

"Oh, that's different," I says; but I found out that most all o' them said "One without" when they meant one no trump.

I looked at my hand; but about all as I had was four hearts, with the king and jack high.

"Pardner," I says, "I don't see nothin' I can bid, unless it'd be one heart. Does that hit you?"

"No talkin' acrost the boards," says Mrs. Garrett. "And besides, one heart ain't over my bid."

So I passed and Mr. Messenger bid two spades. Then my pardner passed and Mrs. Garrett thought it over a w'ile and then bid two without. So I passed again and the rest o' them passed, and it was my first lead.

Well, I didn't have only one spade — the eight-spot — and I knew it wouldn't do my hand no good as long as I couldn't trump in with it; so I led it out. Messenger was dummy, and he laid his hand down. He had about eight spades, with the ace and queen high.

"I might as well take a chance," says Mrs. Garrett, and she throwed on Messenger's ten-spot.

Out come my pardner with the king, and it was our trick.

"What kind of a lead was that?" says Mrs. Garrett to me.

"Pretty good one, I guess," says I. "It fooled you, anyway."

And she acted like she was sore as a boil. Come to find out, she'd thought I was leadin' from the king and was goin' to catch it later on.

Well, her and Messenger took all the rest o' the tricks except my king o' hearts, and they had a game on us, besides forty for their four aces.

"I could of made a little slam as well as not," she says when it was over. "But I misunderstood our friend's lead. It's the first time I ever seen a man lead from a sneak in no trump."

"I'll do a whole lot o' things you never seen before," I says.

"I don't doubt it," says she, still actin' like I'd spilled salad dressin' on her skirt.

It was my first bid next time and hearts was my only suit again. I had the ace, queen and three others.

"Pardner," I says, "I'm goin' to bid one heart and if you got somethin' to help me out with, don't let 'em take it away from me."

"I'll double a heart," says Messenger.

"Oh, somebody else is gettin' cute!" says I. "Well, I'll double right back at you."

"Will you just wait till it comes your turn?" says Mrs. Garrett. "And besides, you can't redouble."

"I guess I can," says I. "I got five o' them."

"It's against our rules," she says.

So my partner done nothin', as usual, and Mrs. Garrett bid one without again.

"I guess you want to play 'em all," I says; "but you'll have to come higher'n that. I'm goin' to bid two hearts."

"Two no trump," says Messenger, and my pardner says "Pass" once more.

"You'll get a sore throat sayin' that," I told her. "Don't you never hold nothin'?"

"It don't look like it," she says.

"Maybe you don't know what's worth biddin' on," I says.

"Maybe she'd better take a few lessons from you," says Mrs. Garrett.

"No," I says, kiddin' her. "You don't want no more female experts in the club or you might have to buy some cut glass once in a w'ile instead o' winnin' it."

Well, I bid three hearts; but Mrs. Garrett come up to three no trump and I couldn't go no higher. This time I led out my ace o' hearts, hopin' maybe to catch their king; but I didn't get it. And Mrs. Garrett copped all the rest of 'em for a little slam.

"If your husband ever starts drinkin' hard," I says, "you can support yourself by sellin' some o' your horseshoes to the Russian government."

It wasn't no lie, neither. I never seen such hands as that woman held, and Messenger's was pretty near as good. In the four deals they grabbed two rubbers and a couple o' little slams, and when they left our table they had over nine hundred to our nothin'.

Mr. Collins and another woman was the next ones to set down with us. The rules was to change pardners and Collins took the one I'd been playin' with. And what does she do but get lucky and they give us another trimmin', though nothin' near as bad as the first one. My pardner, this time, was a woman about forty-eight, and she acted like it was way past her bedtime. When it was her turn to say somethin' we always had to wait about five minutes, and all the other tables was through a long w'ile before us. Once she says:

"You'll have to excuse me to-night. I don't somehow seem to be able to keep my mind on the game."

"No," I says; "but I bet you'd perk up if the lady's prize was a mattress. When you're goin' to be up late you should ought to take a nap in the afternoon."

Well, sir, my next pardner wasn't nobody else but the Missus. She'd started at the fourth table and lost the first time, but win the second. She come along with the husband o 'the pardner I'd just had; so here we was family against family, you might say.

"What kind o' luck you been havin'?" the fella ast me.

"No luck at all," I says. "But if you're any-

wheres near as sleepy as your Missus, I and my
wife should ought to clean up this time."

We didn't. They held all the cards except
in one hand, and that was one my Missus tried
to play. I bid first and made it a no trump,
as they was three aces in my hand. Old Slum-
ber began to talk in her sleep and says: "Two
diamonds." The Missus bid two hearts. Mr.
Sleeper passed, and so did I, as I didn't have
a single heart in my hand and figured the Missus probably had 'em all. She had six, with
the king high and then the nine-spot. Our
female opponent had only two, and that left
five for her husband, includin' the ace, queen
and jack. We was set three.

"Nice work!" I says to the Missus. "You're
the Philadelphia Athletics of auction bridge."

"What was you biddin' no trump on?" she
says. "I thought, o' course, you'd have one
high heart and some suit."

"You don't want to start thinkin' at your
age," I says. "You can't learn an old dog
new tricks."

Mrs. Nap's husband cut in.

"O' course," he says, "it's a man's privilege to call your wife anything you feel like callin' her. But your Missus don't hardly look old to me."

"No, not comparatively speakin'," I says, and he shut up.

They moved on and along come Garrett and Mrs. Messenger. I and Mrs. Messenger was pardners and I thought for a w'ile we was goin' to win. But Garrett and the Missus had a bouquet o' four-leaf clovers in the last two deals and licked us. Garrett wasn't supposed to be as smart as his wife, but he was fox enough to keep biddin' over my Missus, so as he'd do the playin' instead o' she.

It wasn't till pretty near the close o' the evenin's entertainment that I got away from that table and moved to Number Two. When I set down there it was I and Mrs. Collins against her husband and Mrs. Sleeper.

"Well, Mrs. Collins," I says, "I'll try and hold some good hands for you and maybe I can have two helpin's o' the meat when we come to your house."

The other lady opened her eyes long enough to ask who was winnin'.

"Oh, Mrs. Garrett's way ahead," says Mrs. Collins. "She's got a score o' somethin' like three thousand. And Mr. Messenger is high amongst the men."

"Who's next to the leadin' lady?" I ast her.

"I guess I am," she says. "But I'm three hundred behind Mrs. Garrett."

Well, the luck I'd just bumped into stayed with me and I and Mrs. Collins won and moved to the head table. Waitin' there for us was our darlin' hostess and Messenger, the two leaders in the pennant race. It was give out that this was to be the last game.

When Mrs. Garrett realized who was goin' to be her pardner I wisht you could of seen her face!

"This is an unexpected pleasure," she says to me. "I thought you liked the third table so well you was goin' to stay there all evenin'."

"I did intend to," I says; "but I seen you up here and I heard you was leadin' the league, so I thought I'd like to help you finish in front."

"I don't need no help," she says. "All I ast is for you to not overbid your hands, and I'll do the rest."

"How many are you, Mrs. Garrett?" ast Mrs. Collins.

"Thirty-two hundred and sixty," she says.

"Oh, my!" says Mrs. Collins, "I'm hopeless. I'm only twenty-nine hundred and forty-eight. And how about you, Mr. Messenger?"

"Round thirty-one hundred," he says.

"Yes," says Mrs. Garrett, "and I don't believe any o' the rest o' the men is within five hundred o' that."

"Well, Messenger," I says, "if the men's prize happens to be a case o' beer or a steak smothered in onions, don't forget that I'm payin' you thirty-five a month for a thirty-dollar flat."

Now, I'd of gave my right eye to see Mrs.

Collins beat Mrs. Garrett out. But I was goin'
to do my best for Mrs. Garrett just the same,
because I don't think it's square for a man to
not try and play your hardest all the time in
any kind of a game, no matter where your sym-
pathies lays. So when it come my turn to bid
on the first hand, and I seen the ace and king
and four other hearts in my hand, I raised Mrs.
Collins' bid o' two diamonds, and Mrs. Garrett made it two no trump and got away with
it. On the next two deals Messenger and Mrs.
Collins made a game, and Mrs. Garrett got
set a trick once on a bid o' five clubs. The way
the score was when it come to the last deal, I
figured that if Mrs. Collins and Messenger
made another game and rubber, the two wom-
en'd be mighty close to even.

Mrs. Garrett dealt 'em, and says:

"One without."

"Two spades," says Mrs. Collins.

Well, sir, they wasn't a spade in my hand,
and I seen that if Mrs. Collins got it we was
ruined on account o' me not havin' a trump.

And w'ile I wanted Mrs. Collins to win I was
goin' to do my best to not let her. So I says:

"Two without."

"You know what you're doin', do you?" says
Mrs. Garrett.

"What do you mean, know what I'm doin'?"
I says.

"No talkin' acrost the boards," says Messenger.

"All right," I says; "but you can depend on
me, pardner, not to throw you down."

Well, Messenger passed and so did Mrs.
Garrett; but Mrs. Collins wasn't through.

"Three spades," she says.

"Three without," says I.

"I hope it's all right," says Mrs. Garrett.

"I'll tell you one thing," I says; "it's a whole
lot all-righter than if she played it in spades."

Messenger passed again and ditto for my
pardner.

"I'll double," says Mrs. Collins, and we let
it go at that.

Man, oh, man! You ought to seen our genial hostess when I laid down my cards! And heard her, too! Her face turned all three colors o' Old Glory. She slammed her hand down on the table, face up.

"I won't play it!" she hollers. "I won't be made a fool of! This poor idiot deliberately told me he had spades stopped, and look at his hand!"

"You're mistaken, Mrs. Garrett," I says. "I didn't say nothin' about spades."

"Shut your mouth!" she says. "That's what you ought to done all evenin'."

"I might as well of," I says, "for all the good it done me to keep it open at dinner."

Everybody in the room quit playin' and rubbered. Finally Garrett got up from where he was settin' and come over.

"What seems to be the trouble?" he says. "This ain't no barroom."

"Nobody'd ever suspect it o' bein'," I says.

"Look what he done!" says Mrs. Garrett. "He raised my no-trump bid over three spades without a spade in his hand."

"Well," says Mr. Garrett, "they's no use gettin' all fussed up over a game o' cards. The thing to do is pick up your hand and play it out and take your medicine."

"I can set her three," said Mrs. Collins. "I got seven spades, with the ace, king and queen, and I'll catch her jack on the third lead."

"And I got the ace o' hearts," says Messenger. "Even if it didn't take a trick it'd make aces easy; so our three hundred above the line gives Mrs. Collins a score of about ten more'n Mrs. Garrett."

"All right, then," says Garrett. "Mrs. Collins is entitled to the lady's prize."

"I don't want to take it," says Mrs. Collins.

"You got to take it," says Garrett.

And he give his wife a look that meant business. Anyway, she got up and went out o' the room, and when she come back she was smilin'. She had two packages in her hand, and she give one to Messenger and one to Mrs. Collins.

"There's the prizes," she says; "and I hope you'll like 'em."

THREE WITHOUT, DOUBLED

Messenger unwrapped his'n and it was one o' them round leather cases that you use to carry extra collars in when you're travelin'. Messenger had told me earlier in the evenin' that he hadn't been outside o' Chicago in six years.

Mrs. Collins' prize was a chafin'-dish.

"I don't blame Mrs. Garrett for bein' so crazy to win it," I says to her when they couldn't nobody hear. "Her and Garrett both must get hungry along about nine or ten P. M."

"I hate to take it," says Mrs. Collins.

"I wouldn't feel that way," I says. "I guess Mrs. Garrett will chafe enough without it."

When we was ready to go I shook hands with the host and hostess and says I was sorry if I'd pulled a boner.

"It was to be expected," says Mrs. Garrett.

"Yes," I says; "a man's liable to do most anything when he's starvin' to death."

The Messengers and Collinses was a little ways ahead of us on the stairs and I wanted we should hurry and catch up with 'em.

"You let 'em go!" says the Missus. "You've spoiled everything now without doin' nothin' more. Every time you talk you insult somebody."

"I ain't goin' to insult them," I says. "I'm just goin' to ask 'em to go down to the corner and have a drink."

"You are not!" she says.

But she's just as good a prophet as she is a bridge player. They wouldn't go along, though, sayin' it was late and they wanted to get to bed.

"Well, if you won't, you won't," says I. "We'll see you all a week from to-night. And don't forget, Mrs. Collins, that I'm responsible for you winnin' that chafin'-dish, and I'm fond o' welsh rabbits."

I was glad that we didn't have to go far to our buildin'. The Missus was pleasant company, just like a bloodhound with the rabies. I left her in the vestibule and went down to help Mike close up. He likes to be amongst friends at a sad hour like that.

THREE WITHOUT, DOUBLED

At breakfast the next mornin' the Wife was more calm.

"Dearie," she says, "they don't neither one of us class as bridge experts. I'll admit I got a lot to learn about the game. What we want to do is play with the Hatches every evenin' this week, and maybe by next Tuesday night we'll know somethin'."

"I'm willin'," I says.

"I'll call Mrs. Hatch up this forenoon," she says, "and see if they want us to come over there this evenin'. But if we do go remember not to mention our club or tell 'em anything about the party."

Well, she had news for me when I got home.

"The San Susies is busted up," she says. "Not forever, but for a few months anyway. Mrs. Messenger called up to tell me."

"What's the idear?" I says.

"I don't know exactly," says the Missus. "Mrs. Messenger says that the Collinses had boxes for the opera every Tuesday night and the rest didn't feel like goin' on without the

Collinses, and they couldn't all o' them agree on another night."

"I don't see why they should bust it up on account o' one couple," I says. "Why didn't you tell 'em about the Hatches? They're right here in the neighborhood and can play bridge as good as anybody."

"I wouldn't think o' doin' it," says she. "They may play all right, but think o' how they talk and how they dress!"

"Well," I says, "between you and I, I ain't goin' to take cyanide over a piece o' news like this. Somehow it don't appeal to me to vote myself dry every Tuesday night all winter—to say nothin' o' two dollars a week annual dues to help buy a prize that I got no chance o' winnin' and wouldn't know what to do with it if I had it."

"It'd of been nice, though," she says, "to make friends with them people."

"Well," I says, "I'll feel a little more confident o' doin' that if I see 'em once a year—or not at all."

THREE WITHOUT, DOUBLED

IV

I can tell you the rest of it in about a minute. The Missus had became resigned and everything was goin' along smooth till last Tuesday evenin'. They was a new Chaplin show over to the Acme and we was on our way to see it. At the entrance to the buildin' where the Messengers lives we seen Mr. and Mrs. Hatch.

"Hello, there!" says the Wife. "Better come along with us to the Acme."

"Not to-night," says Mrs. Hatch. "We're tied up every Tuesday evenin'."

"Some club?" ast the Missus.

"Yes," says Mrs. Hatch. "It's a bridge club—the San Susie. The Messengers and Collinses and Garretts and us and some other people's in it. Two weeks ago we was to Collinses', and last week to Beardsleys'; and to-night the Messengers is the hosts."

The Missus tried to say somethin', and couldn't.

"I been awful lucky," says Mrs. Hatch. "I win the prize at Collinses'. It was a silver pitcher—the prettiest you ever seen!"

The Missus found her voice.

"Do you have dinner, too?" she ast.

"I should say we do!" says Mrs. Hatch. "And simply grand stuff to eat! It was nice last week at Beardsleys'; but you ought to been at Collinses'! First, they was an old-fashioned beefsteak supper; and then, when we was through playin', Mrs. Collins made us welsh rabbits in her chafin'-dish."

"That don't tempt me," I says. "I'd just as soon try and eat a raw mushrat as a welsh rabbit."

"Well, we got to be goin' in," says Hatch.

"Good night," says Mrs. Hatch; "and I wisht you was comin' with us."

The pitcher we seen was called *The Fly Cop*. Don't never waste a dime on it. They ain't a laugh in the whole show!

THE END